"YOU THINK THIS IS FUNNY?" ANGEL DEMANDED.

Without warning, the door of the storage cage slammed shut.

He watched in disbelief as Kendra bolted it.

"I think it's funny *now*," she mocked him.

Angel leapt to the door, shaking it viciously, trying to break the lock.

"That girl," Kendra said. "The one I saw you with before—"

Buffy . . .

"You stay away from her!"

"I'm afraid you are not in a position to threaten."

Angel pressed his face to the metal gate. "When I get out of here I'll do more than threaten—"

"Then I suggest you move quickly," Kendra replied, glancing at a row of high windows that ran along one wall of the storage cage. Uneasily, Angel followed her eyes.

"Eastern exposure," Kendra explained. "The sun comes in a few hours." A smile touched her lips. "More than enough time for me to find your girlfriend."

Buffy, the Vampire Slayer™

BUFFY

THE VAMPIRE

SLAYER™

THE ANGEL CHRONICLES
Vol. 2

A novelization by Richie Tankersley
Based on the hit TV series created by Joss Whedon
Based on the teleplays "Halloween" by Carl Ellsworth,
"What's My Line, part 1" by Howard Gordon & Marti Noxon
and "What's My Line, part 2" by Marti Noxon

AN ARCHWAY PAPERBACK
Published by POCKET BOOKS
New York London Toronto Sydney Tokyo Singapore

This book is a work of fiction. Names, characters, places and incidents are products of the author's imagination or are used fictitiously. Any resemblance to actual events or locales or persons, living or dead, is entirely coincidental.

AN ARCHWAY PAPERBACK *Original*

An Archway Paperback published by
POCKET BOOKS, a division of Simon & Schuster Inc.
1230 Avenue of the Americas, New York, NY 10020

™ and copyright © 1999 by Twentieth Century Fox Film Corporation. All rights reserved.

All rights reserved, including the right to reproduce this book or portions thereof in any form whatsoever. For information address Pocket Books, 1230 Avenue of the Americas, New York, NY 10020

ISBN: 0-671-02627-5

First Archway Paperback printing January 1999

10 9 8 7 6 5 4 3 2 1

AN ARCHWAY PAPERBACK and colophon are registered trademarks of Simon & Schuster Inc.

Printed in the U.S.A.

IL: 9+

to Martin
    soulmate
    kindred spirit
    and friend for all seasons
        je t'aime toujours
        Madeline

THE ANGEL CHRONICLES
Vol. 2

THE CHRONICLES:

PROLOGUE

Angel was growing restless.

He'd been waiting since eight o'clock, his gaze fixed on the steady flow of people in and out the front door of the Bronze. She should have been here by now. She should have been here more than an hour ago.

Buffy, he thought. *Buffy, are you okay?*

He could feel his senses growing even sharper, his mind groping out across the room. The Bronze was busy tonight, as usual—noisy and crowded with its mobbed dance floor, loud band, and general confusion of conversation and fun. Yet, sitting alone at his table, Angel felt strangely distant from it all.

He'd been in many places like this over the course of his life. And though the fashions and music, the language and etiquette might have changed from century to century, there was still that seductive play

1

of light and shadow across the floor, across the walls; there was still that enticing crush of too many bodies packed into too small a space. Even now he could smell it—that throbbing heat of human flesh pressing in on him from every side. And he closed his eyes, surrendering to the long-ago memories that came flooding back.

Yes, he'd been in places just like this many times before. Waiting for victims. Waiting for women . . .

But none of them like Buffy.

Slowly he opened his eyes.

Surrounded by people, he felt utterly alone. Surrounded by laughter, he felt weary with an age-old sadness. He looked around at all the young faces, so full of innocence and recklessness and life. He felt pity for them. And he envied them.

They were part of Buffy's world.

A world where he'd never belong.

Angel clasped his hands together, his jaw tightening in a grimace. *Why did I even come tonight, anyway?* He'd promised himself a thousand times that he'd walk away from Buffy and never look back. Hadn't he felt enough pain and regret in his lifetime without dragging her into it, too? Love was a dangerous emotion—it weakened people, clouded their instincts, made them vulnerable. Love was a luxury neither of them could afford if they wanted to survive.

He stared down at the table. There was a peculiar warmth inside him whenever he thought of her . . . a warmth that flowed through his veins like something sacred and pure. Yes, he admitted to himself, loving

Buffy made him vulnerable. But it also made him feel more completely alive than he'd ever felt throughout his long, endless lifetime.

She should be here by now, he thought again.

He lifted his dark eyes and fixed them anxiously upon the door.

THE FIRST CHRONICLE:

HALLOWEEN

PROLOGUE

Only two days left until Halloween.

Darkness had fallen over Sunnydale, and the pumpkin field had closed its gates for the night.

Now a brisk fall wind rattled the scarecrows and cornstalks along the fence and shook the strings of colored lights draped festively overhead. Dead leaves swept across the ground, over piles of straw and bales of hay, beneath an old wooden wagon with its equally old wooden sign: Pop's Pumpkin Patch. Grinning jack-o-lanterns flickered eerily through the shadows.

And the vampires were restless.

Buffy hit the ground with a thud, feeling a jack-o-lantern smash beneath her. Breathlessly, she rolled to one side, grabbed a smaller pumpkin, and hurled it at the approaching vampire as he leaned in for the kill. The pumpkin caught him full in the face, throwing him off balance, and before he could recover himself, a second pumpkin hit him between the eyes.

The vampire stumbled backward. Instantly Buffy whipped out a wooden stake and threw it straight at his heart, but he managed to grab a scarecrow, using it as a shield. There was a dull thud as the stake pierced the chest of the scarecrow. The vampire grinned delightedly.

"Hmmm." So this wasn't going to be as easy as she'd thought. And after she'd made *other* plans for tonight—much more *important* plans than battling demons and rolling around in jack-o-lantern muck.

This whole situation was *really* beginning to annoy her.

As the vampire tossed the scarecrow aside, Buffy jumped to her feet and resumed her defensive posture. For several minutes she stubbornly held her ground, until two sidearm blows and a merciless kick sent her back down again. She was so busy fighting, she didn't even realize she was being watched— watched and filmed through a video camera a safe distance away.

Hidden among the outlying trees and shadows of the pumpkin patch, another vampire was taping the whole messy combat. *Had* been taping, in fact, ever since it first began. Recording Buffy's uncanny speed as she rebounded, recording her incredible strength as she delivered two hard uppercuts and a kick to her opponent's jaw.

Yes, the creature thought, *this is exactly what we needed* . . .

He frowned as he noticed the blinking light in the

corner of his viewfinder. The battery was getting low, and the fight wasn't finished. Grunting, he gave the camera a frustrated shake, then refocused it.

Buffy had gained the upper hand at last. A vicious head butt and a swift kick to the vampire's chest sent him sprawling headlong into a mountain of pumpkins, where Pop's Pumpkin Patch sign toppled to the ground. With one smooth movement, Buffy grabbed the sign and swept it under the vampire's feet, knocking him off balance. Then she plunged the pointed end deep into his heart.

The night was still.

A line of static burst across the video camera, but the hidden vampire kept on shooting.

He managed to get the pile of dust that had once been Buffy's antagonist; he managed to get Buffy standing up and walking away . . .

And then the video went out.

The creature stepped from the shadows, the camera still held to his eyes. He moved slowly forward and lowered the camera from his hideous face.

He smiled, pleased with his efforts.

Then he, too, disappeared into the night.

CHAPTER 1

Another ten minutes, Angel decided. *I'll give her another ten minutes . . .*

For the last half hour he'd kept his attention focused on the doorway, but now, more and more unsettling thoughts were weighing on his mind.

Maybe Buffy was in trouble. Not that she couldn't defend herself, he reasoned, but nightly patrols were always potentially disastrous. Or maybe she hadn't been able to sneak out of the house tonight. Or maybe she'd made other plans and simply forgotten about their date.

Angel sighed. Oblivious to the partying all around him, he sat there and brooded.

"I *know.* Is the Bronze not-happening or what?"

Angel glanced up to see Cordelia standing beside him. With her long dark hair, skintight clothes, and perfect figure, she knew she looked sultry and confident as always. To her annoyance, however, Angel didn't seem to be noticing.

"Um, hi," he said. "I'm waiting for Buffy."

"Great!" Sitting down, Cordelia made herself comfortable, leaning forward a little to reveal her plunging neckline. "I'm supposed to be meeting Devon, but he's nowhere to be seen. It's like he thinks being in a band gives him an obligation to be a flake. Well, his loss is your incredible gain . . ."

She droned on and on. Angel managed a thin smile and drummed his fingers nervously on the table. He gave her his halfhearted attention, trying to be polite.

That was why he didn't see Buffy come in a few minutes later. He didn't see the sheepish look on her face, or how she stopped to catch her breath, or how she ran her hands self-consciously through her hair, pulling out dirt and seeds and pumpkin slime. Scanning the crowd, Buffy spotted Angel and Cordelia at their table, and felt her heart plunge. It was obvious Cordelia was in full-flirt mode. Buffy watched her chattering and laughing, and after awhile, Angel shook his head and laughed, too.

Buffy looked down at her own filthy clothes. She looked back at Cordelia's carefully planned perfection. And then miserably she turned away.

"So then I told Devon," Cordelia rambled on, "you call *that* a leather interior? My Barbie Dream Car had nicer seats."

Angel laughed again, rather painfully. And then he noticed Buffy at last.

"Buffy?" He got up and hurried toward the club entrance, leaving Cordelia hanging in midsentence.

Buffy saw him coming and stopped. *Too late now.* Steeling herself, she put on her best game face.

"Oh. Hi," she greeted him cheerfully. "I'm—"

"Late," Angel said. He appraised her with one swift glance while Buffy managed a nod.

"Rough day at the office," she mumbled.

Smiling, Angel pulled a piece of straw gently from her hair. "So I see."

He handed it to her. Humiliated, Buffy tried to turn it into a joke.

"Hey, it's a look. A seasonal look."

"Buffy." Cordelia sashayed past them, an obvious smirk on her sensual lips. "Love your hair. It just *screams* street urchin."

Inwardly Buffy cringed. Outwardly, she tried once more to sound casual.

"You know what?" she told Angel. "I need to go . . . put a bag over my head."

But Angel wasn't fooled. As he looked down at her troubled expression, his voice softened. "Don't listen to her. You look fine."

"You're sweet." Buffy managed a grim smile. "A terrible liar. But sweet."

Turning again to leave, she felt Angel's hand on her arm.

"I thought we had . . . you know."

"A date?" Buffy turned back to him now, all her resolve suddenly crumbling. Her voice was quiet but tight with emotion. "So did I. But who am I kidding?

Dates are things normal girls have. Girls who have time to think about nail polish and facials and stuff. You know what I think about? Ambush tactics. Beheading. Not exactly the stuff dreams are made of."

Angel stared down at her, feeling her pain, not knowing quite what to say. As he watched her go, Cordelia glided up to him again, holding out two cups of coffee. She smiled a triumphant smile.

"Cappuccino?"

CHAPTER 2

Volunteers Are Winners, the signs read. Safe and Sane Halloween.

The halls of Sunnydale High were thronged with students moving to and from class. Halloween decorations were plastered everywhere, and a long table had been set up, manned by several kids and their neat rows of sign-up sheets. Principal Snyder stood by, arms clamped across his chest, beady eyes surveying the crowd. He looked even sneakier than usual today. It was obvious he was on the prowl.

An unsuspecting girl almost made it past the table before he grabbed her.

"Hey!" she exclaimed. She tried to wriggle free, but his grip was relentless.

"You're volunteering," he ordered.

"But I have to get to class—"

His grip tightened even more. He steered her over

to the sign-up table just as Buffy, Willow, and Xander walked by with curious stares.

"Snyder must be in charge of the volunteer safety program for Halloween this year," Willow observed.

Xander hunched his shoulders, hands dug deep into his pockets. "Note his interesting take on the 'volunteer' concept," he said dryly.

Buffy warily eyed the table. "What's the deal?"

"A bunch of little kids need people to take them trick-or-treating," Xander explained, sounding less than thrilled. "Sign up and you get your very own pack of sugar-hyped runts for the night."

"Yikes. I'll stick to vampires—"

Buffy broke off as a hand fell to her shoulder. Principal Snyder was looking down at her with an undisguised sneer.

"Ms. Summers. Just the juvenile delinquent I've been looking for."

"Principal Snyder," Buffy said, trying to sound polite. She always found it really hard to keep a straight face around the man. With his balding head and huge ears, he looked amazingly like a troll.

"Halloween must be a big night for you, huh?" the principal continued sarcastically. "Tossing eggs. Keying cars. Bobbing for apples. One pathetic cry for help after another. Well. Not this year, missy."

Before Buffy could respond, he walked her firmly over to the table, Xander and Willow reluctantly following.

"Gosh, I'd love to volunteer," Buffy said, her mind racing for an excuse, "but I recently developed . . .

carpal tunnel syndrome and, tragically, I can no longer hold a flashlight."

Principal Snyder handed her a pen. Willow began to look worried.

"The program starts at four, and the children have to be home by six," he instructed.

Buffy stared down at a long list of names.

Xander and Willow stared at each other, and then at the pens Principal Snyder handed each of them.

They signed.

"I can't believe this," Xander grumbled, as the threesome headed into the school lounge. "We have to dress up and the whole deal?"

"Snyder said costumes were mandatory," Willow sighed.

Buffy forced a rueful smile. "Great. I was going to stay in and veg. It's the one night a year that things are supposed to be quiet for me."

"Halloween quiet?" Xander shot her a quizzical look. "I figured it would be a big old vamp scare-a-palooza."

"Not according to Giles. He swears that tomorrow night is, like, dead for the undead. They stay in."

"Those wacky vampires." Xander shook his head. "That's what I love about 'em. They just keep you guessing."

He stopped at the drinks machine while Buffy and Willow found a table. Dropping in some change, he waited for his soda to come out, but nothing happened.

He hit the machine with his fist. He gave the machine a few choice insults. Then he hit it again.

"Harris!" A voice boomed out.

Xander looked up to see a large meaty hand descending on his shoulder. It belonged to Larry, a mean-tempered moose of a jock, and not one of Xander's personal favorites.

"Larry," Xander said casually. "Looking very cromag as usual. What can I do you for?"

Larry glanced over to where Buffy and Willow were sitting. The two girls were engaged in a private conversation, totally unaware of the attention they were getting.

Larry leaned in closer to Xander. "You and Buffy— you're just friends, right?"

Xander was quick. "I like to think of it less as a friendship and more as a solid foundation for future bliss—"

"So she's not your girlfriend?" Larry broke in impatiently.

"Alas, no."

"You think she'd go out with me?"

"Well, Lar, that's a hard question to . . . no. Not a chance."

"Why not? I heard some guys say she was fast."

Xander could feel himself bristling. "I hope you mean in the 'like the wind' sense."

"You know what I mean."

Larry was actually leering at him now, and Xander's anger erupted. He grabbed Larry by his T-shirt, pulling him down to eye-level. "That's my friend you're talking about," Xander said.

Larry was not impressed and definitely not intimidated. In fact, Xander's outburst not only amused him, it pumped him up for battle. With a cocky smile, he stretched himself to his huge fullness.

"Oh, yeah? What are you going to do about it?"

Xander stood his ground. "I'm going to do what any man would do about it," he stammered. "Something . . . damn manly."

With one massive heave, he tried to shove Larry into the soda machine but hardly budged him an inch. Grimacing, he saw Larry draw back a fist and aim it at his face, and Xander bravely steeled himself to be mutilated.

But the blow never came. At the last second, another hand suddenly intercepted, grabbing Larry's wrist, snapping it back from Xander's face. In a flash, Buffy spun Larry around, pinned his arms behind him, and slammed him hard into the drinks machine.

A free soda dropped out.

"Get gone," Buffy said.

As Larry scurried away, she picked up the Dr. Pepper and gave a pleased smile. "Ooh. Diet."

And then it dawned on her that Xander hadn't moved. Hadn't said a word. That he was just standing there staring at her in total shock and disbelief.

"Do you know what you just did?" he finally exploded.

Buffy thought a minute. "Saved a dollar?"

"Larry was about to pummel me!" Xander exclaimed.

"Oh, that." Buffy brushed it off. "Forget about it."

Xander glared at her, positively fuming. "I will," he

snapped at her. "Maybe fifteen, twenty years from now. When my rep for being a *sissy-man* finally fades."

Buffy's mouth opened in surprise. "Xander—"

"A black eye heals, Buffy," he threw at her. "But cowardice has a nearly unlimited shelf-life. But thanks. Thanks for your help."

As Xander stomped off, Buffy and Willow exchanged knowing looks.

"I think I just violated the guy code," Buffy confessed. "Big time."

She took her seat again as Willow sighed and nodded.

"Poor Xander. Boys are so fragile." Then, brightening, Willow asked, "Speaking of—how was your date last night?"

"Misfire." Buffy frowned. "I was late due to unscheduled slayage. Showed up looking trashed."

"Was he mad?"

"Actually, he seemed pretty un-mad. Which may have had to do with the fact that Cordelia was drooling in his cappuccino."

Willow gave her a reassuring smile. "Buffy, Angel would never fall for her act."

"You mean that 'actually showing up, wearing a stunning outfit, embracing personal hygeine' act?"

"You know what I mean. She's not his type."

"Are you sure? I mean, I don't really know what his type is." Buffy sounded frustrated and a little sad. "I don't know his turn-ons and turn-offs or his idea of the perfect evening. I've known him less than a year and he's not one to over-share."

Willow listened sympathetically. "True. It's too bad we can't sneak a look at the Watcher Diaries and read up on Angel. I'm sure it's full of fun facts to know and tell."

Buffy stared at Willow. *Watcher Diaries!* In the back of her mind she could feel her thoughts spinning, a plan already beginning to form.

"Yeah, it's too bad," Buffy said casually. "That stuff is private."

"Also, Giles keeps them in his office. In his personal files."

Buffy's voice lowered, a conspiratorial whisper. "Most importantly," she said, "it would be *wrong.*"

CHAPTER 3

The library was empty.

As Buffy and Willow peeked through the library doors, they couldn't hear a single sound from inside.

The two girls looked at each other.

Then, slowly, Buffy began tiptoeing into the room, leaving Willow to stand guard at the open doorway.

The diaries would be in Giles's office, Buffy reminded herself, so that's where she headed now. *In and out again, no problem at all.* She was so intent on her mission that she didn't even see Giles emerging from the book cage behind her.

"Buffy," Giles said. "Excellent."

Buffy jumped as though she'd been shot. She spun around to face him, her voice unnaturally shrill. "Nothing! Hi."

She could see Giles staring at her, giving her one of

his odd looks. And then he shrugged, his mind going neatly back on track.

"I wanted to talk to you about tomorrow night," he said, carrying a stack of books over to the table. "As it should be calm, I thought we might work on new battle techniques—"

Buffy cut him off. "You know, Giles, you're scaring me now." She glanced back toward the door. *"You* need to have some fun."

She moved deliberately closer as he began sorting through his books. And then, as slyly as she could, she motioned Willow to come in.

Willow's eyes widened in alarm. She shook her head adamantly and mouthed *no!,* but Buffy only motioned again, more insistently this time. Resigned, Willow took a deep breath and started working her way into the library, creeping silently behind Giles's back.

"There's this amazing place you can go and sit down in the dark," Buffy rushed on, trying to hold Giles's attention. "And there are these moving pictures. And the pictures tell a *story*—"

Giles raised an eyebrow in her direction. "Ha, ha. Very droll. I'll have you know I have many relaxing hobbies."

"Such as?"

"Well." He'd been leafing through one of the heavy volumes, but now he stopped, obviously struggling for an answer. "I'm very fond of cross-referencing."

Buffy shook her head at him. "Do you stuff your own shirts or do you send them out?"

Without warning Giles closed the book he was holding. He took one step, as though to go to his office. Panicked, Willow froze in her tracks. Buffy's mind raced, determined to keep him occupied.

"So, how come Halloween is such a yawner?" she asked quickly. "Do the demons just hate how commercial it's become?"

It worked. Giles looked at her.

"Well, it's interesting—" Giles began.

Willow was almost to the door of his office now. As Giles started to pick up his stack of books, Buffy grabbed the one on top, moving off to his other side to divert his attention.

"But not, I suspect, to you." Giles frowned suspiciously, taking the book away from her. "What is it you're after?"

Again Willow froze. They were definitely caught this time, she just *knew* it.

"Well, of course it's of interest!" Buffy insisted passionately. "I'm the Slayer! I need to know this stuff! You can't keep me in the dark anymore!"

Again Giles started to pick up his stack of books. Buffy grabbed his arm.

"Look at me when I talk to you!" she blurted out.

"Buffy," Giles was beginning to sound annoyed, "I don't have time to play games—"

"Ms. Calendar said you were a babe!"

Giles stopped. Buffy smiled. From the other side of the room, Willow rolled her eyes, giving Buffy a "shame on you, that's so low," expression.

For a long moment there was silence.

Then at last Giles looked back at Buffy, his calm

demeanor obviously flustered. "She said what?" he asked softly.

Willow slipped into his office and began gathering up the diaries.

"She said," Buffy stammered, "you know, that you were hot. A hunk of burning something or other. So. What do you think of that?"

"I, well . . ." Giles took off his glasses and began fiddling with them. "Um, I don't—a burning hunk of what?"

"You know," Buffy made a face, "gross as it is for me to contemplate you grownups having smootchies, I think you should go for it."

Relieved, she saw Willow and the diaries slip out of the office and head swiftly for the door. Mission accomplished. Except Giles was still staring at her, and she still had to escape.

"Buffy," he said, slipping his glasses back on, "I appreciate your interest, but—"

"I've overstepped my bounds!" Buffy agreed quickly. "It's none of my business. My God, *what* was I thinking? Shame. *Shame.* Gotta go."

She bolted from the library and disappeared down the hall, leaving Giles to gaze after her in complete bewilderment.

Several minutes crept by.

"A babe?" Giles mumbled to himself.

And then he smiled.

"I can live with that."

Safe in the women's restroom, Buffy and Willow sat side by side on the sinks, huddled over the Watcher

Diaries. They'd never seen anything quite so fascinating, and as Willow flipped slowly through the books, Buffy suddenly rested her finger on one of the pages.

"Man," Buffy breathed, "look at her."

What they saw was a detailed drawing of a woman. An incredibly beautiful woman with long dark hair and a flowing eighteenth-century gown.

"Who is she?" Willow asked.

"It doesn't say. But the entry is dated seventeen-seventy-five."

"Angel was eighteen," Willow mused. "And still human."

Buffy gave a tight smile. "So this was the kind of girl he hung around. She's pretty . . . coifed."

"She looks like a noblewoman or something," Willow noted, "which means being beautiful was sort of her job."

"And clearly, this girl was a workaholic. Willow, I'll never be like this . . ."

Willow heard the mixture of hurt and longing in Buffy's voice. "Come on," she said reassuringly, "she's not that pretty. She's got a funny waist. See how tiny it is?"

Buffy gave her a withering look. "Now I feel better. Thanks."

"No, really," Willow tried to redeem herself, "she's like a freak. A circus freak. Yuck."

But Buffy wasn't listening. Instead her mind was flowing back, back into some long-ago mysterious past where Angel had been young and mortal.

"It must have been wonderful," Buffy said dreamily. "To put on some fantabulous gown and go to a ball, like a princess, to have servants and horses and yet more gowns . . ."

Willow hesitated. "Yeah. Still, I think I prefer being able to vote. Or I will, when I can."

The bathroom door opened, jarring Buffy from her reverie. She looked up to see Cordelia sweeping over to the mirrors.

"So, Buffy," Cordelia pulled lipstick out of her purse and leaned in to check her reflection. "You ran off and left poor Angel by his lonesome last night. I did everything I could to comfort him."

Buffy's tone was grim. "I bet."

"What's his story, anyway? I mean, I never see him around."

"Not during the day, anyway," Willow mumbled.

Cordelia stopped doing her lips. She turned to Buffy now, almost reluctantly. "Please don't tell me he still lives at home. Like he has to wait until his dad gets home to take the car?"

Buffy shook her head. "I think his parents have been dead for, um, a couple hundred years."

"Oh, good. I mean—what?"

"He's a vampire, Cordelia," Buffy said flatly. "I thought you knew."

Cordelia stared, taking this all in. Then she calmly put her makeup back in her purse.

"Oh. He's a vampire. Of course. But the cuddly kind. Like a Care Bear with fangs."

"It's true," Willow insisted calmly.

Cordelia crossed her arms tightly over her chest. "You know what I think? You're trying to scare me off because you're afraid of the competition." She paused, then added smugly, "Look, Buffy, you may be hot stuff when it comes to demonology or whatever, but when it comes to dating, *I'm* the Slayer."

She turned and flounced out of the bathroom.

And Buffy watched her leave, not wanting to admit how deeply those words had stung.

CHAPTER 4

Even though Ethan's Costume Shop was musty and rundown, it was stocked with every sort of costume imaginable.

Today the place was packed. Kids of all ages rummaged through hangers and shelves, through boxes and bags, searching for that one perfect Halloween costume. The supply seemed endless.

Buffy walked up and down between rows of clothing and hats and masks, searching for something to wear. No matter how hard she tried, she just couldn't seem to muster any Halloween spirit. She moved almost mechanically through the mass of excited shoppers, wishing someone would just cancel Halloween this year, or at the very least, wishing she could just spend it in bed.

She glanced up as Willow came toward her, and she

tried her best to sound enthusiastic. "What did you find?"

"A time-honored classic," Willow said proudly.

She watched as Willow pulled a costume from a bag. The package read Ghastly Ghost, and it showed a person covered with a large white ghost sheet, complete with eye holes, ghostly smile, and the word *boo* stenciled across the chest.

"Willow," Buffy managed to hide her amusement, "can I give you a little friendly advice?"

Willow looked worried. "It's not spooky enough?"

"It's just, you're never going to get noticed if you keep hiding," Buffy tried to explain. "You're missing the whole point of Halloween."

"Free candy?"

"It's come as you *aren't* night. The perfect chance for a girl to get sexy and wild with no repercussions."

"I don't get wild." Willow's eyes grew wide and solemn. "Wild on me equals spaz."

Buffy firmly disagreed. "You've got it in you, Will. You're just scared—"

She broke off as Xander walked over. She could tell he was still mad at her, and Willow eagerly took advantage of the opportunity to change the subject.

"Hey, Xander. What did you get?"

He opened his shopping bag. He pulled out an orange plastic machine gun.

"That's not a costume," Buffy informed him.

"I've got some fatigues from the Army surplus at home," Xander explained. And then, in a poor attempt at Schwarzenegger, he added, "Call me the two-dollar costume king, baby."

Buffy took a deep breath and plunged in. "Hey, Xander, about this morning. I'm really sorry—"

"Do you mind, Buffy? I'm trying to repress."

"I promise I'll let you get pummeled from now on."

Xander paused. He could never stay mad at anyone for very long.

"Thank you," he said at last. "Okay. Actually, I think I could have—"

He broke off, realizing that Buffy's attention had wandered far away from the matter at hand.

"Hello?" Xander prompted her. "That was our touching reconciliation you just left."

"Sorry," Buffy murmured. "It's just . . . look at that."

Xander and Willow both turned around. They followed the direction of Buffy's gaze to the wall at the back of the store.

The red gown was draped over a mannequin. Fashioned in an elegant eighteenth-century style, it hung to the floor in flowing folds of satin and lace. The front of the skirt showed a narrow swath of pink, decorated along each side with small dainty bows, while even more delicate lace accentuated the low square neckline and cascaded down from the sleeves.

Willow drew in her breath.

It looked exactly like the gown in the Watcher Diaries.

Buffy seemed to be mesmerized. Without taking

her eyes from the dress, she moved slowly, almost cautiously, toward it, Willow and Xander following.

"It's amazing," Willow whispered, while Xander firmly shook his head.

"Too bulky. I prefer my women in spandex."

Buffy stopped in front of the gown. Gingerly she lifted one hand, about to touch the dress, when a man suddenly approached them from a rear doorway.

Ethan Rayne was the owner of the shop. Tall and unassumingly dressed, there was still an air of understated sophistication about his clothes and a quiet hint of elegance about the man himself. His eyes reflected a devilish sort of glint. His smile was soft and somewhat secretive, and when he spoke, his voice held just a trace of British accent.

"Please." He stopped beside Buffy. He reached out for the gown. "Let me."

Buffy shook her head in wonder. "It's—"

"Magnificent," he said. "I know."

Carefully he removed it from the mannequin. Almost reverentially he held it up to her.

"My," Ethan Rayne murmured. "Meet the hidden princess."

And indeed, Buffy seemed magically transformed. Even Willow and Xander, the two who knew her best, couldn't help staring in silent awe. She was stunningly beautiful.

"I think we've made a match," Ethan purred. "Don't you?"

As though emerging from a spell, Buffy stepped away and reluctantly shook her head. "I'm sorry. There's no way I can afford this."

"Nonsense," Ethan soothed. "I feel quite . . . moved to make you a deal you can't refuse."

Buffy's whole face brightened. "Really?"

Again she pressed the gown to her heart; again she turned back to the mirror.

Ethan Rayne smiled.

CHAPTER 5

The old factory had long been abandoned.

It sat within thick shadows in a dark, dangerous part of town, and no one had ventured inside its cavernous walls for years and years.

Only the rats had been brave enough to infest its ugly, rotting interior.

Until, of course, the vampires came.

"Here it comes," said Spike.

The room he stood in was washed with pale blue light. This light glowed from a bank of televisions lining one wall, and it threw everything into eerie distortion, including Spike's white hair and the delicate bones of his face. As Spike watched intently, an identical image suddenly flickered to life on every single screen.

The image was Buffy.

The recording was of her fight in the pumpkin patch.

Spike watched the film with single-minded concentration. Behind him stood the vampire who had taped it, who had hidden himself last night where Buffy couldn't see.

Now on the television screen, Buffy was falling onto the jack-o-lantern, crushing it beneath her. Now she was getting up again, now she was hurling a smaller pumpkin at her attacker.

"Rewind that," Spike said. "I want to see it again."

Yet he couldn't stay still to watch it. He paced the room restlessly, keen eyes narrowed, his senses absorbing every detail of the tape.

"She's tricky." Spike sounded amused, almost pleased. "Baby likes to play."

The video ran again. This time Spike noted the part where Buffy used the wooden sign to stake the vampire.

"See that? Where she stakes him with that thing?" Spike's admiration was obvious. "That's what you call resourceful."

He paced. He paused.

"Rewind it again."

A voice spoke behind him then. A soft silky voice, a haunting blend of dreamy seduction and childlike innocence.

"Miss Edith needs her tea," the voice said.

Spike didn't need to turn around to know that Drusilla had wandered in with one of her dolls, that she was standing there, swaying slightly, clutching it tight against her chest. And it didn't matter how many centuries he'd spent adoring her—each time Drusilla came near him, it was love all over again.

"Come here, poodle."

As always, his voice seemed to change when he spoke to Drusilla, growing protective somehow, almost tender. Yet even as he welcomed her, he kept his attention focused on the video and on Buffy.

Drusilla wafted over to him. He slipped his arms around her frail shoulders.

"Do you love my insides?" Drusilla murmured. "The parts you can't see?"

"Eyeballs to entrails, my sweet. That's why I have to study this Slayer. Once I know her, I can kill her. And once I kill her, you can have your run of Sunnyhell and get strong again."

"Don't worry," Drusilla assured him. "Everything's switching. Outside to inside." She opened her mouth, growling softly at his neck. "It makes her weak."

Spike's head came up at once. He proceeded with caution. "Really. Did my pet have a vision?"

"Do you know what I miss?" Drusilla pouted. "Leeches."

"Come on," Spike urged, laughing softly. "Talk to daddy. This thing that makes the slayer weak. When is it?"

"Tomorrow."

"But tomorrow is Halloween. Nothing happens on Halloween."

Drusilla shook her head. "Someone's come to change it all."

She tilted her head back into the shadows.
"Someone new," she whispered.

Ethan's Costume Shop had closed for the night.
The last customer had finally gone, but the store was not quite deserted.
A tall figure moved silently into the back room.
A tall figure wearing a long, hooded black robe.
Ethan Rayne stopped beside an altar. One by one he lit the black candles that encircled it.
Directly in front of him, in the very center of the circle, was a marble bust of a woman. Her features were beautiful and serene. Kneeling before her, Ethan began to speak, squeezing his hands tightly closed, then opening them again.
His palms began to bleed. They bled thickly and freely, from stigmatalike wounds on his hands.
"The world that denies thee, thou inhabit," Ethan chanted. "The peace that ignores thee, thou corrupt."
He dabbed his blood upon his eyelids. He smeared a bloody cross upon his forehead.
"Chaos," he murmured. "As ever, I am your faithful, degenerate son."
He knew the true power of the statue.
He knew it, and he called upon it now.
For the back of the statue was quite different from the front.
It wasn't beautiful, nor was it peaceful to look at.
It was a hideously horrifying male visage.
A mask of pure evil.

CHAPTER 6

Halloween day dawned crisp and clear.

There was a feeling of unrepressed excitement in the air, and classes let out early so that student volunteers could go home and change into their costumes.

Buffy stood in her bedroom, gazing silently at her reflection in the mirror.

She was wearing the gown from Ethan's Costume Shop, and for a moment she almost wondered if she'd actually stepped back in time. Her hair—a brunette wig—was piled elegantly on top of her head. Held in place with an old-fashioned comb, it still fell loose in a few stray tendrils that curled around her face. Around her neck hung a lovely jeweled necklace, making her throat seem all the more delicate. Even to herself she looked like something from a fairy tale. She'd never felt so beautiful.

Like the woman in the diary, she thought. *Like the women Angel had loved . . .*

"Where are you meeting Angel?" Willow's voice floated out from the bathroom, bringing Buffy back to earth.

"Here. After trick-or-treating. Mom's gonna be out."

"Does he know about your costume?"

"Nope. Call it a blast from his past. I'll show him I can coif with the best of 'em!" Buffy smiled at her reflection, then added, "Come on out, Will. You can't stay in there all night."

"Okay," Willow sounded resigned. "But don't laugh."

"I won't—"

Buffy's words caught in her throat. As Willow emerged from the bathroom, Buffy stared at her friend's amazing transformation. Willow was wearing makeup, and her hair was pinned in a casual upsweep. A clingy dark, midriff-baring top, leather miniskirt, knee-high boots—Willow was a total rocker babe. Totally gorgeous. And obviously totally miserable.

"Wow." Buffy was practically speechless.

Willow took one look at her plunging neckline, grabbed her ghost sheet, and turned back for the bathroom.

"Will," Buffy reached out and stopped her. "You're a dish. I mean, really—"

"But this just isn't me," Willow argued.

"That's the point! Halloween is the night that *not* you is you, but not *you*, you know?"

Willow was still pondering this as the doorbell rang

"That's Xander," Buffy announced. "You ready?"

Willow paused, gave a deep sigh. "Yeah. Okay."

She tried to smile, but Buffy wasn't fooled. Willow reminded her of a deer caught in someone's headlights. She clamped her arms tightly around her exposed midriff. Terror supreme.

"Cool!" Buffy reassured her. "I can't wait to watch the boys go nonverbal when they see you."

She ran downstairs and opened the front door. True to form, Xander was wearing his low-rent army costume—camouflage pants and jacket, tank tee, aviator sunglasses—and carrying his plastic gun.

He stepped up to Buffy and saluted. "Private Harris. Reporting for—"

And then his words choked off. As he got a close-up look at Buffy, his mouth dropped open and his hand fell to his side.

"Buffy." He bowed his head. "My Lady of Buffdom. The Duchess of Buffonia. I am in awe. I completely renounce spandex."

"Thank you, kind sir." Buffy curtsied. "But wait till you see—"

"Hi," Willow said from the staircase behind them.

Expectantly they both turned.

Willow was standing there, covered head to toe with her ghost sheet.

"Casper," Buffy finished lamely.

Xander stared at Willow's costume, trying to come up with a compliment. "Hey, Will," he said brightly, "that's . . . that's a fine *boo* you have there."

Willow hung her head.

She could feel Buffy's disappointment as the three of them went out the door.

CHAPTER 7

THE ANGEL CHRONICLES

Outside Sunnydale High, kids were being dropped off by the dozens, screaming and shouting and waving their trick-or-treat bags as they stampeded into the building. Inside, the hallways swarmed with fierce little demons and goblins, while students valiantly tried to separate them into manageable groups.

"Where's your bodyguard, Harris? Curling her hair?"

Xander heard Larry coming before he actually saw him. When he turned around, Larry was swaggering toward him, dressed as a pirate and brandishing a plastic sword. Featuring baggy shorts, T-shirt, fake scars, and eye patch, Larry's costume was even less inspired than Xander's.

Xander glared at him. Larry made a sudden jerking movement with his sword, and Xander instinctively flinched. Laughing, Larry walked off.

Xander lifted his machine gun and took careful aim at Larry's back. His finger itched on the trigger, but after several seconds, he lowered the gun again in disgust. Even with a plastic toy, he couldn't quite bring himself to shoot.

Farther down the corridor, Principal Snyder was leading a small group of children over to Buffy. As she quickly scanned their eager faces, she couldn't help noticing that there was a vampire among them.

"Here's your group, Summers." Principal Snyder gave her his usual sneer. "No need to speak to them—the last thing they need is your influence. Just bring them back in one piece and I won't expel you."

Buffy returned his look with one of her own. As he walked away, she leaned over to the kids with a smile.

"Hi," she began, then noticed Principal Snyder standing a few feet away. Scowling at her.

Around the corner, Oz was kneeling on the floor by his locker, carefully inspecting his guitar. Glancing up, he saw Cordelia marching up to him in a skintight leopard leotard, cat ears, mittens, and drawn-on whiskers.

"Oz. Oz."

Oz waited, calmly assessing her.

"Cordelia," he finally said. "You're like a great big cat."

"That's my costume," Cordelia returned impatiently. "Are you guys playing tonight?"

"At the Shelter Club."

Cordelia raised her chin haughtily. "Is mister 'I'm the lead singer I'm so great I don't have to show up for a date or even call' gonna be there?"

"Yeah," Oz deadpanned, standing up. "You know, he's just going by Devon now."

Cordelia wasn't amused. "Well, you can tell him that I don't care, and that I didn't even mention it and I didn't even see you so that's just fine."

Oz continued to stare at her. He gave a slight nod. "So *what* do I tell him?"

"Nothing!" Cordelia exploded. "Jeez, get with the program."

Furiously she stalked off, leaving Oz unimpressed and completely unperturbed.

"Why can't I meet a nice girl like that?" he mumbled to himself.

Standing up, he turned and bumped right into Willow, who was still covered with her ghost sheet.

"Sorry," Oz said, trying to untangle himself.

"Sorry," Willow replied, trying to help him.

"Sorry."

"I'm sorry."

Flustered, Willow moved on. Oz stood and watched her a moment, then headed off in the opposite direction.

At the end of the hallway, Xander was lecturing his own little group of trick-or-treaters.

"Okay," Xander informed them officiously. "On sleazing extra candy. Tears are the key. Tears'll usually get you a double-bagger. You can also try the old 'you missed me' routine, but it's risky. Only go there for chocolate." He paused, letting his instructions sink in. "Understood?"

The kids all nodded.

"Good." Xander straightened and squared his shoulders. "Troops, let's move out."

Within minutes, Xander's group had joined the others outside. While student volunteers hurried to keep up, costumed children raced eagerly from house to house, their delighted squeals and make-believe screams echoing through the neighborhood. They were all having so much fun, time practically flew by, and before they knew it, the streets had grown darker and spooky with shadows.

As Buffy's weary group returned from a house, she couldn't help noticing their dejected expressions.

"What'd Mrs. Davis give you?" she asked them, concerned.

They opened their hands to show her. They were holding brand new toothbrushes.

Buffy sounded indignant. "She must be stopped." She herded the kids together and steered them down the sidewalk. "Let's hit one more house. We still have a few minutes before we've got to get back."

Perking up, the children ran off again, leaving Buffy to smile at their enthusiasm. She was glad she'd been roped into doing this, after all—the evening had turned out to be much more fun than she'd ever imagined.

She had no way of knowing that the fun was about to end.

That at this very moment, in the back room of Ethan's Costume Shop, a black-hooded figure was kneeling before a row of black candles, reciting an incantation.

"Janus, hear my plea." Ethan Rayne spoke the words, but he spoke them now in Latin. *"Take this night as your own. Come forth and show us your truth."*

Buffy felt an inexplicable shiver go through her.

At the house on the corner, kindly Mrs. Parker came to the front door, smiling and handing out candy to the group of giggling monsters. Willow waited patiently for them at the end of the porch. The wind was starting to pick up, and the chill in the air had grown noticeably sharper. She huddled into her ghost sheet, wishing she'd dressed warmer underneath.

"Trick or treat!" the children shouted.

"Oh, my goodness," Mrs. Parker beamed at them. "Aren't you adorable!"

In the costume shop, Ethan picked up the statue, his hands leaving bloody prints upon the stone. His face dripped with sweat, his body trembled feverishly. And then, again in Latin, he chanted, *"The mask is made flesh. The heart is curdled by your holy presence. Janus, this night is yours!"*

Buffy ushered her kids quickly down the block. A sudden gust of wind sent a second, deeper shudder down her back. She stopped, frowning.

Something wasn't right.

At the house on the corner, Mrs. Parker was looking down at the plastic pumpkin in her hands. She shook her head in utter dismay.

"Oh, dear," she mumbled. "Am I all out? I could have *sworn* I had some candy left."

In Ethan's Costume Shop, the candles went out.

The only light now was the one emanating from the hideous statue, casting a sickly green glow through the shadows.

Ethan Rayne lowered his hood.

A satisfied grin spread slowly across his face.

"Show time," he whispered.

THE ANGEL CHRONICLES

CHAPTER 8

Mrs. Parker looked down at the trick-or-treaters clustered around her. Miniature demons, vampires, gargoyles, and witches—they were all staring at her and at her empty candy container.

"I'm sorry, Mr. Monster," Mrs. Parker sighed, playing along. "Maybe I—"

She never got to finish her apology. Without warning, a slimy green hand caught her by the throat and yanked her forward. As she tried desperately to scream, she could see that the hand belonged to the make-believe gargoyle.

Except he wasn't make-believe anymore.

Where a costumed child had stood only seconds before, there was now a *real* gargoyle. As horribly real as the rest of the creatures swarming over her porch.

Willow couldn't believe what was happening. "Let her go!" she cried, trying to reach Mrs. Parker.

A horned demon deliberately blocked her way. As the demon turned and attacked the gargoyle, Mrs. Parker was finally able to break free and scramble inside to safety, locking the door behind her.

"What—" Willow mumbled. "What's—"

She tried to back off the porch. She felt dizzy and weak and strange. Stumbling, she gasped for breath. Her eyes grew wide with terror. The next instant she fell to the ground, her body limp and lifeless beneath its sheet.

The whole neighborhood was in chaos.

From every street, sidewalk, and corner came shrieks of terror, car alarms, cries for help, sounds of running, howling, the shatter of breaking glass. The air was thick with panic and the smell of fear.

As hysterical children raced past him for cover, Xander turned in confusion and immediately de-shouldered his plastic machine gun. For a split second he felt a peculiar dizziness throughout his whole body. Staggering a little, he tried to keep his balance, then just as quickly felt the dizziness leave him, clearing his head once more.

His posture went ramrod straight.

He raised his gun.

Not the plastic gun he'd held only a moment ago, but a fully functional M-16 machine gun.

Xander didn't even look surprised. His demeanor now was all military, his jaw set, his eyes like steel.

In front of Mrs. Parker's house, Willow felt herself sit up. She still felt peculiar, not quite herself, but at least the awful dizziness had gone. She stood slowly, trying to remember exactly what had happened. And then she looked down at her feet.

"Oh. Oh my God . . ."

She was still lying there on the porch.

Or, at least, her *ghost* was.

Willow stared at the ghost sheet, at the lifeless form that lay beneath it. And then she looked down at her own clothes.

The Willow standing here was wearing a miniskirt and halter top—the rocker-babe costume that Buffy had picked out for her. But the Willow lying there wasn't moving at all—in fact, the standing Willow could see her own boots submerged in the sleeping Willow, as though the two of them were still precariously connected.

Willow's voice was barely a whisper. "I'm a . . . I'm a real ghost."

Machine gun fire sounded behind her. Willow turned to see Xander backing across the street, surveying the area in silent panic.

"Xander!"

As joy and relief swept through her, Willow raced over to her old friend. But to her dismay, Xander whipped around and pointed his gun straight at her.

"Xander, it's me. Willow!"

Xander eyed her suspiciously. He cautiously lowered his gun.

"I don't know any Willow," he said.

"Quit messing around, Xander," Willow pleaded. "This is no time for jokes."

Xander's stare was cold. "What the hell is going on here?"

"You don't know me?" Willow peered earnestly into his face, but there wasn't a hint of recognition.

"Lady, I suggest you find cover."

"No, wait!" Before Xander could walk away, Willow stepped in front of him. But instead of stopping him as she intended, an incredible thing happened.

She felt Xander pass right through her.

Pass right through and step out from her other side.

Willow gazed down at herself in disbelief. She was trembling from the contact, a rush of pure physical pleasure enveloping her from head to toe.

"Ooh," she breathed.

Xander, on the other hand, freaked out. Spinning around, he raised his gun and pointed it at her again.

"What are you?" he demanded.

"Xander." Willow raised both of her hands where he could see them. "Listen to me. I'm on your side, I swear. Something crazy is happening. I was dressed as a ghost for Halloween, and now I *am* a ghost. You were supposed to be a soldier, and now, I guess, you're a real soldier—"

"And you expect me to believe that?" Xander snapped.

Before Willow could answer, a little vampire emerged from the bushes, growling at them. Immediately Xander took aim.

"No!" Willow yelled. "No guns. That's still a little kid in there."

"But—"

"No guns. That's an order. Let's just get—" She broke off, spotting something down the street. "Buffy!"

Buffy was indeed coming toward them, stumbling along the sidewalk in her gown. At once Willow ran to meet her, leaving Xander to grudgingly follow.

"Buffy, are you okay?"

As Willow approached her, she heard another menacing growl from the bushes—only louder this time—more like a roar. Behind them, the little vampire had been joined by a very large demon, and the two of them were heading this way.

Buffy stood between Willow and Xander, several paces behind.

The three of them watched as the monsters got closer.

Xander scowled. "This could be a situation."

"Buffy, what do we do?" Willow asked desperately.

Buffy's eyes grew wide.

And then she fainted.

CHAPTER 9

Without a word or a single sound, Buffy just dropped to the sidewalk and lay there.

Willow stared down in disbelief.

Xander hoisted his gun and fired above the demons' heads. As the monsters took off, he turned back to Willow, who was kneeling beside Buffy and coaxing her back to consciousness.

"Buffy! Are you all right?"

"What?" Buffy whispered.

"Are you hurt?" Xander asked.

"Buffy, are you hurt?" Willow echoed.

Buffy gazed up at them. Her face was blank. "Buffy?"

"She's not Buffy," Willow said to Xander.

Xander frowned. "Who's Buffy?"

"Oh, this is fun," Willow sighed. And then to Buffy, "What year is this?"

Buffy thought a moment. "Seventeen-seventy-five, I believe. I don't understand. Who are you?"

Xander helped her up. Willow gave her a reassuring smile.

"We're friends," Willow said.

"Friends of whom?" Buffy was in obvious distress. "Your dress is . . . everything is strange." As her panic rose, she cried, "How did I come to be here?"

Willow tried to soothe her. "Okay, breathe, okay? You're gonna faint again." She paused to glance at Xander. "How are we supposed to get through this without the Slayer?"

Xander stared. "What's a Slayer?"

Without warning a demon jumped Buffy from behind. Where the old Buffy would have pulverized it with one punch, this new Buffy simply screamed and batted at it with her fingers. Instead of helping, Willow could only watch in utter amazement. The demon pulled at Buffy's wig, but it had become her real hair now, coming loose in the struggle, cascading down around her bare shoulders. It was Xander who finally stepped in, butting the demon with his rifle until it gave up and ran off.

Xander turned solemnly to Willow. "I suggest we get inside before we run into any other—"

"Demon!" Buffy shrieked. "A demon!"

Willow and Xander whirled to defend themselves. Bewildered, they saw only a car driving toward them along the street. Buffy promptly dived into Xander's arms, shrinking against him and hiding her face.

"It's not a demon," Willow tried to explain. "It's a car."

"What does it want?" Buffy whimpered.

Xander fixed Willow with a level stare. "Is this woman insane?"

"She's never seen a car," Willow said.

"She's never seen a car."

"She's from the past," Willow said.

"And you're a ghost."

"Yes. Now let's get inside."

Xander stood for a moment, considering. And then he finally looked over at Willow.

"I just want you to know I'm taking a lot on faith here," he informed her. "Where do we go?"

"Where's the closest . . ." Willow shook her head, trying to think. "Uh, we can go to a friend's house."

A short time later the three of them piled through the back door into Buffy's kitchen. Safe for the time being, Xander locked up the house, then stood at the window to keep guard. Buffy's eyes wandered over the countertops and appliances, totally overwhelmed by the mysterious objects around her.

"I think we're clear," Xander announced.

"Hello!" Willow called. "Mrs. Summers?" And then, when no one answered, "Good. She's gone."

"Where are we?" Buffy asked.

"Your place," Willow told her. "Now we just need to—"

There was a violent pounding on the front door. Startled, they froze for an instant, then began moving through the house, Xander in the lead, Willow close behind, Buffy trailing. In the dining room, Buffy stayed behind, while Xander and Willow bravely continued on.

"Don't open it!" Willow warned him.

Xander hesitated. "It could be a civilian."

"Or a mini-demon."

The pounding stopped.

They stopped, too, and waited.

At last Xander crossed to a window to look out. In the dining room Buffy saw something sitting on the mantel and walked over to examine it.

It was a picture.

A picture of a young woman who looked amazingly like her.

Buffy picked it up, deeply puzzled, as Willow approached her.

"This," Buffy whispered, "this could be me."

"It is you," Willow insisted. "Buffy, can't you remember at all?"

"No, I . . . I don't understand any of this, and I . . ." Buffy hesitated, studying the photograph once more. "This is some other girl, I would never wear this . . ."

She was whining now, and rambling, dangerously close to tears. Willow stared at her in disbelief.

"This low apparel," Buffy pouted, "and I don't like this place, and I don't like you, and I just want to go *home!*"

"You *are* home!" Willow told her.

Buffy began to cry. The pounding started again. Terrified, Buffy shrieked.

Even Willow was beginning to feel the strain of Buffy's helplessness. "You couldn't have dressed up like Xena," she grumbled, hurrying back to Xander.

She was just in time to see a demonic hand smash through the window beside Xander's head. The thing grabbed at him, but Xander managed to jump back just in time.

"Not a civilian," Willow observed.

Xander gave a curt nod. "Affirmative."

He stuck his gun out the window.

"Hey!" Willow reminded him sharply. "What'd we say?"

Xander ignored her. There was a short burst of gunfire, then they both heard the demon scampering away.

Xander's look was self-righteous. "Big noise scare monster. Remember?"

"Got it," Willow conceded.

But what they heard now was a terrified scream. It came from somewhere outside, and as Xander peered out the window again, his muscles tensed for action.

"Hey—!"

Before Willow could stop him, he raced out the front door. Buffy came up behind Willow, her voice bordering on hysteria.

"Surely he'll not desert us?" Buffy fretted.

Willow had had enough. She gave Buffy a look, shrugged her shoulders and walked away. "Whatever . . ."

Out in the darkness, Xander had located the source of the screaming. Cordelia was running frantically down the street, her costume torn, her hair a disheveled mess. There were scratches on her face. Several yards behind her a huge hairy creature was relentlessly catching up.

Xander headed toward her. Cars had been abandoned in the streets, and shadowy figures were still running in the distance, some of them on the prowl, others fleeing for their lives. As Xander reached her, Cordelia screamed and tried to fight him off, before suddenly realizing who he was.

"Xander?"

"Come inside," Xander ordered her. He didn't have the slightest idea who she was.

He rushed her toward the house. He practically threw her inside, slamming the door behind them.

"Cordelia!" Willow exclaimed.

Cordelia looked supremely irritated. "What's going on?"

"Okay," Willow hurried to explain, "your name is Cordelia, you're not a cat, you're in high school, we're your friends—well, sort of."

"That's nice, Willow," Cordelia cut her off. "And you went mental *when?*"

Willow's face lit up. "You know us?"

"Yeah, lucky me. What's with the name game?"

"A lot's going on," Willow admitted.

"No kidding. I was just attacked by JoJo the dogfaced boy. Look at my costume! Think Party-Town's gonna give me my deposit back? Not on the likely."

As she was spouting off, Cordelia suddenly noticed a large rip up the side of her leotard. Xander had obviously noticed it, too, for he took off his jacket and put it around her.

"Here," Xander said.

Surprised, Cordelia stared at his pumped biceps, at the tatoo she'd never seen there before. She glanced over and realized Willow was staring at the exact same thing.

"Thanks," she murmured.

Willow forced herself back to the moment. "Okay. You three stay here while I get help. If something tries to get in, just fight it off."

"It's not our place to fight," Buffy protested fearfully. "Surely some men will come and protect us?"

Cordelia regarded her in total disgust. "What's *that* riff?"

"It's like amnesia, okay?" Willow sighed. "They don't know who they are. Just sit tight."

She didn't have time to go into it now. She hurried by Cordelia and heard the girl say, "Who died and made her the boss?" And then she passed straight through the wall behind Cordelia's back.

She didn't notice Spike out in the street.

Didn't notice him standing there amid the chaos, his long black coat drawn around him, his face a cruel vampire face. And yet his eyes shone as wide and bright as a child's on Christmas morning.

"Well," Spike smiled, taking everything in. "This is just . . . *neat.*"

CHAPTER 10

The night crept by.

Willow hadn't returned yet, and Xander was growing more and more restless.

He pushed a table against a window. He proceeded to check all the smaller windows, as well, just to make sure they were secure. Buffy followed him around like a puppy, not wanting to be alone.

"Surely there's somewhere we can go?" she begged him. "Some safe haven?"

Xander wouldn't be swayed. "The lady said stay put." He glanced at Cordelia and added, "Check upstairs. Make sure everything's locked."

Confused by Xander's answer, Buffy started in on him again. "You would take orders from a woman? Are you feeble in some way?"

"Ma'am," Xander sighed, "in the army we have a saying. Sit down and shut the—whoa."

His voice broke off. He was staring down at the floor where a photograph had fallen, one which clearly showed the three of them—he and Buffy and Willow—together. He stared at it for a long time, and then he looked up at Buffy.

"She must be right," he said to her. "We must have some kind of amnesia."

Buffy drew herself up indignantly. "I don't know what that is, but I'm sure I don't have it. I bathe quite often."

"How do you explain this?" he demanded, indicating the photo.

Buffy lifted her nose into the air. "I don't! I was brought up as a proper lady. I'm not meant to understand things. I'm just meant to look good and then someone nice will marry me. Possibly a baron."

"This isn't a tea party, princess," Xander retorted. "Sooner or later you're going to have to fight."

"Fight?" Buffy looked appalled. "These low creatures? I'd sooner die."

"Then you'll die."

"Oh, good," a voice spoke out from behind them. "You guys are all right."

They turned to see Angel hurrying in from the kitchen.

He shook his head at them in amazement.

"It's total chaos out there," he said.

Buffy and Xander stared at him.

"Who are you?" they asked.

Alone in the library, Giles was immersed in his book catalog. He was used to the silence in here, especially after school hours, so when the faint screams and sirens sounded in the faraway distance, he lifted his head and frowned.

Then he remembered. Of course, it was Halloween. Screams and sirens would be the norm tonight.

But had that noise just then been something else? A stranger, softer sound—one much closer by?

Again Giles looked up, pausing to listen, thinking perhaps he'd imagined it.

A growl?

Slowly he turned from his work.

He didn't hear the sound at all now. Still, he supposed it wouldn't hurt to investigate—

He was turning around when Willow ran out at him without warning, straight through the library wall.

Giles let out a yell.

He jumped back, arms flailing, knocking into shelves and sending books flying in all directions.

Willow stood there sheepishly. She held up one hand.

"Hi," she said.

"Okay," Angel said, "does somebody want to fill me in?"

He stared at Buffy's old-fashioned dress, the lowcut neckline, the delicate lace. Something stabbed at his memory, and for one split second he felt as though he were falling back through time, through centuries . . .

Xander's voice yanked him roughly back to the present. "Do you live here?"

"No! You know that. Buffy . . ." Bewildered, Angel took a step toward her. It *was* Buffy, he was certain, and yet somehow, *not* Buffy at all. *Someone I knew, someone forgotten a long time ago* . . . "I'm lost here," he mumbled. "You . . ."

Buffy drew back fearfully. Angel squinted at her long dark wig.

"What's up with your hair?" he asked.

"They don't know who they are," Cordelia said impatiently, coming back downstairs. "Everyone's become a monster. It's a whole big thing." She stopped and collected herself. She gave Angel a smile. "How are you?"

Pounding erupted all around them. As the lights went out, plunging the room into total blackness, Buffy shrieked and grabbed Cordelia.

"Do you mind?" Cordelia snapped, shoving her away.

Xander turned to Angel. "Take the princess here and secure the kitchen. Catwoman, you're with me."

Cordelia gratefully handed Buffy over to Angel and followed Xander into the living room.

"But I don't want to go with you!" Buffy protested, trying to wrench from Angel's grasp. "I like the man with the musket."

"Come on," Angel ordered her.

Buffy's voice was tiny and hopeful. "Do you have a musket?"

She clung to him as they entered the kitchen. The back door was standing wide open, and Angel slowly shook his head.

"I didn't leave that open."

He moved cautiously and silently toward the door. Fearful, Buffy watched him as she cowered back against the wall. She didn't hear the cellar door opening right beside her. She didn't notice the vampire slinking out from the shadows . . .

Angel shut the back door and turned around.

"Look out!" he yelled.

As Buffy spun, the vampire grabbed at her. Amazingly, she managed to seize the door and slam it back on the creature's arm. But the vampire was much more powerful than she was. Almost immediately it flung the door wide again, sending Buffy sprawling to the foor. Angel made a dive for the creature, tackling it and wrestling it into the dining room. As Buffy staggered to her feet, she looked around frantically for a weapon. Taking a big knife from the counter, she peered timidly through the doorway and saw Angel on top of the vampire, his back to her, struggling to hold the creature down.

"A stake!" Angel yelled.

"What?"

"Get me a stake!"

Without warning he turned in her direction, and Buffy screamed.

Angel's face was contorted, hideous, an enraged vampire face. Buffy screamed again and raced out the back door.

"Buffy, *no!*" Angel shouted.

It was just the opportunity his opponent needed.

Throwing Angel off, the other vampire twisted free and came around on top of him.

Giles still wasn't certain he'd entirely recovered from his shock. But, as he'd soon learned from

Willow, there was plenty of work to be done tonight if they wanted to save Sunnydale.

Now the two of them were surrounded by piles and piles of books. Looking for something—*anything*—that might give them a clue as to what was happening this wild, unforgettable Halloween.

Willow gazed at Giles in frustration. "I don't even know what to look for. Plus," she added lamely, glancing down at her ghost arm, "I can't turn the page."

"Right." Giles nodded understandingly. "Okay, then, let's review. At sundown, everyone became whatever they were masquerading as."

"Right. Xander was a soldier, and Buffy was an eighteenth-century girl."

Giles took off his glasses. He stared blandly at Willow's outfit. He raised both eyebrows.

"And your costume?"

"I'm a ghost," Willow said.

A faint smile played over Giles's mouth as he took in her very non-ghost attire. "Yes, but a ghost of *what,* exactly?"

Willow shifted, embarrassed about the midriff-baring top and leather miniskirt. "This is nothing," she defended herself. "You should have seen what Cordelia was wearing. A *unitard.* And these little cat things. Ears and stuff."

"Good heavens. Cordelia became an actual feline?"

Willow stared back at Giles. Something was beginning to nag at her, far back from a corner of her mind.

"No," Willow said slowly. "She was still the same old Cordelia, just in a cat costume."

She crossed her arms over her midriff. Giles looked at her, his brow furrowed deep in thought. He put his glasses on again.

"She didn't change," Giles repeated.

"No." And it was coming to Willow now, finally, in a delayed burst of realization. "Hold on," she said excitedly. "Party-Town. She told us she got her outfit from Party-Town—"

"And everybody who changed, where did they acquire their costumes?"

"We all got ours at this new place," Willow said. "Ethan's."

There was no time to lose.

CHAPTER 11

"**H**ello?" Giles called softly. "Is anyone in?"

Not that they'd really expected to find anyone inside Ethan's Costume Shop at this late hour. The store was dark, seemingly deserted, and yet Giles and Willow entered easily through the front door.

Yes, Giles thought to himself, *almost too easily.*

Together they moved slowly through the main room. Costumes were strewn everywhere. Masks lay about on the floor and countertops, like so many severed heads. Mannequins stood within the shadows, and Willow had the distinct feeling they were watching her with flat, painted eyes. She was bravely trying to quell her overactive imagination when she noticed the open doorway in the back of the shop.

Almost at once Willow spotted the altar and the ring of black candles, the golden statue—its hideous, evil face, the glowing green eyes . . .

"Giles. . . ." she whispered.

Giles came up behind her, following the direction of her stare.

"That's Janus," he said. "A mythical Roman god."

"What does it mean?"

"Primarily, it represents the division of self." His eyes went anxiously from corner to corner. "Male and female. Light and dark—"

"Chunky and creamy style." Ethan's mocking voice was terrifyingly close. "No, sorry. That's peanut butter."

He stepped out from a shadow, smiling at Giles.

Giles stared back at him, his own face tight with shock.

"Willow," Giles said firmly. He stepped in front of her, never taking his eyes off Ethan. "Get out of here. Now."

"But—"

"Now, Willow."

Giles seldom used that tone with any of them. And when he did, Willow knew all too well that he was deadly serious.

She turned and bolted from the room.

Now Ethan Rayne and Giles stood face to face.

"Hello, Ethan."

"Hello, *Ripper,*" Ethan replied.

A dangerous silence fell between them.

Eerie green light played over Giles's face, accentuating its tenseness, its grim determination—and yet Ethan's manner was light. He was clearly enjoying this.

Enjoying every minute.

"What, no hug?" he taunted Giles. "Aren't you happy to see your old mate?"

Giles remained composed. "I'm surprised I didn't guess it was you. This Halloween stunt *stinks* of Ethan Rayne."

"It does, doesn't it?" Ethan replied proudly. He picked up a Halloween mask, rubbing his fingers almost lovingly over the surface. "Not to blow my own horn, but it's genius. The very embodiment of 'be careful what you wish for.'"

"It's sick," Giles returned. "And brutal. It harms the innocent—"

"Oh, and we all know that *you* are the champion of innocence and all things pure and good, Rupert," Ethan went on condescendingly. He paused, then, "This is quite an act you've got going here, old man."

Giles's shoulders stiffened. "It's no act. It's who I am."

"It's who you are? The *Watcher?* Sniveling tweed-clad guardian of the Slayer and her kin?"

Ethan's smile was cold. His tone grew even more mocking.

"I think not. I know who you are. And I know what you're capable of." And then something seemed to dawn on him. "But they *don't,* do they?" he realized. "They have no idea where you come from."

Ethan finally got the reaction he'd hoped for. It was obvious from Giles's expression that he felt threatened by this new line of attack. Only this time his mild demeanor began to change.

No one in Sunnydale had ever seen this side of Giles.

This was a side he kept hidden. *Had* kept hidden for a long, long time.

"Break the spell, Ethan," he demanded now, advancing slowly. "Then leave this place and never come back."

"Why should I?" Ethan threw back at him. "What do I get in the bargain?"

The answer was deathly calm. "You get to live."

"Ooooh. You're scaring—"

Ethan's words exploded inside his mouth.

As Giles dropped him with a vicious punch, his unfinished sentence oozed out across the floor with his blood.

CHAPTER 12

Xander, Cordelia, and Angel were striding determinedly down the middle of the street.

"You're sure she came this way?" Xander asked.

Angel shook his head. "No."

He'd had enough time now to change back into human form, but the damage had already been done. He knew Buffy had a significant head start on them. Secretly he wondered if they'd find her too late, or even at all.

Cordelia tried to be upbeat. "She'll be okay."

"*Buffy* would be okay," Angel reminded her. "Whoever she is now, she's helpless. Come on."

The three of them hurried faster, past Spike's hiding place in the shadows. A small demon and an equally small vampire hovered at his side.

"Do you hear that, my friends?" Spike murmured happily. "Somewhere out here is the tenderest meat you've ever tasted. And all we have to do is find her *first.*"

Buffy was terrified.

Lost and alone, she wandered through unfamiliar streets in an unfamiliar century, her clothes and shoes muddied and torn beyond repair. Without knowing it, she had entered the industrial section of town, that place of forgotten factories and boarded-up warehouses, where even the lowest of life never dared venture.

She struggled through an alleyway, trying to climb over heaps of boxes and trash. Her eyes darted fearfully around her. Shadows crouched on every side, black and endless as nightmares. And when someone stepped out in front of her, blocking her way, she was so panic-stricken she couldn't even scream.

The pirate was gigantic. He towered high above her, eyes glittering in the darkness, leering down at her with a lascivious, black-toothed grin.

"Pretty . . . pretty . . ." he chuckled deep in his throat.

Larry's pirate costume had seemed ridiculous at the start of the evening.

But now it had become the real thing.

Savagely he jerked Buffy into his arms, laughing as she screamed and tried to twist free. When one of her fingers managed to gouge his good eye, he let out a furious bellow and flung her away.

Buffy hit the ground, stunned and whimpering. She

tried to crawl away, but Larry lifted her to her feet once more.

"No," Buffy pleaded, "no. . . ."

Roughly he grabbed her face. He opened his mouth and ran his tongue slowly along his jagged, scummy teeth.

Then he moved in for a kiss.

With a yell, Xander came out of nowhere, hitting Larry with a flying tackle. As Buffy scrambled away, the two of them went at each other full force.

Buffy ran right into Cordelia.

"Buffy? Are you okay?"

Trembling violently, Buffy threw herself into Cordelia's arms. For once, Cordelia was at a complete loss how to handle the situation. She stood there with Buffy burrowed against her and watched the battle raging several feet away.

Larry had always been strong, but in *this* incarnation, Xander was stronger. As Larry tried to reach for his sword, Xander knocked it away.

Buffy looked up to see Angel hurrying toward them. She shrieked and gripped Cordelia even tighter.

Cordelia ran out of patience.

"What is your deal?" Cordelia snapped at her. "Take a pill!"

"He's . . . he's a *vampire!*" Buffy screamed.

Angel stopped and stared at them. For a split second the concern on his face was touched with deep hurt. Oblivious, Cordelia rolled her eyes. She gave Angel a long-suffering look.

"She's got this thing where she thinks—oh, forget

it," Cordelia told him. Then, in her most patronizing tone, she said sweetly to Buffy, "It's okay. Angel is . . . a *good* vampire. He'd *never* hurt *you.*"

Buffy faltered. "He—really?"

"Absolutely." Cordelia might have been soothing a dim-witted child. "Angel is our *friend.*"

Buffy looked timidly at Angel, still not convinced. As Angel went over to Xander, Xander finished Larry off with a headbutt and two swift punches.

Larry hit the ground, out cold.

For a minute, Xander stared down at him. Then he turned to Angel with a puzzled frown.

"It's strange," Xander said, "but beating up that pirate gave me a weird sense of closure."

"Guys!" Willow shouted.

As the group turned expectantly, they saw Willow coming toward them at a dead run. Angel moved forward, already sensing that things were about to get worse.

"Willow—"

"You guys gotta get inside," Willow said breathlessly.

She pointed behind her, to a cluster of shadowy figures that was making its way in their direction. Angel recognized Spike at once. The others seemed to be an odd asssortment of both child-sized and grown-up monsters.

Xander took control. "We need to triage."

"This way." Angel pointed. "Find an open warehouse."

Xander gallantly rounded up the females. "Ladies, we're on the move."

Everyone took off except Buffy.

In her weakened condition and torn, heavy dress, it was all she could do to even stand up.

With one smooth movement Angel swept her into his arms. Her body was small and fragile against his, and he could feel her overwhelming fear. This was a side of Buffy he'd never seen before.

A dependent side. A helpless side.

A side that would most certainly get her killed.

Angel held her tighter, carrying her swiftly through the winding maze of dark, dangerous streets.

CHAPTER 13

They had to get to safety.

As Xander, Cordelia, and Angel rounded the corner of an alley, Angel shifted Buffy in his arms and motioned to a warehouse door a short distance away.

"Over here!" he shouted.

Together they slid the door open and dashed inside, just as Spike and his minions appeared behind them. With only seconds to spare, they wrestled the door shut again, then looked around frantically for some sort of barricade. Old crates and broken furniture were stacked against one wall. As Xander immediately started moving stuff against the door, he yelled over to Angel.

"Check and see if there are any other ways in!"

Angel was ready for action. "Just stay here," he told Buffy, handing her off to Cordelia.

Cordelia rolled her eyes as Buffy fell into her arms. "Fabu. More clinging."

But the barricade wasn't working.

Xander jumped back as something jerked at the warehouse door. He could see demonic hands punching through it now, tearing it apart.

The door jerked again.

And then it began to slide.

The makeshift barricade flew everywhere. Xander and Angel fell back, retreating with the others as the warehouse door came completely open.

Spike stepped inside, smiling triumphantly at his loyal followers.

Ethan Rayne was smiling, too, even though his bloody face was plastered to the floor.

"And you said 'Rupert the Ripper' was long gone," he taunted.

Giles stood over him calmly. It was a frightening calm, a lethal calm.

Slowly and deliberately he wiped his fingers clean on a white handkerchief.

"How do I stop the spell?" he asked again.

Ethan began to laugh. "Say pretty ple—" he began, but Giles aimed a savage kick at his side, leaving him gasping for breath. "Janus," Ethan finally managed. "Break the statue."

Immediately Giles grabbed it and threw it against the wall. And then, as the statue shattered into pieces, he turned back again to Ethan.

For a long, long while Giles gazed down at the floor.

He was alone in the room now.

Ethan had disappeared.

As Giles and Ethan were having their standoff, Spike was enjoying one of his own.

Angel and Xander were pinned now, held at bay by Spike's minions, and though the two of them fought to free themselves, no one could help Buffy now.

"Look at you," Spike murmured softly. He moved toward Buffy as she backed away, his pacing slow and stealthy, his look deceptively kind. He could see how absolutely petrified she was, her eyes desperate and full of tears. Excitement raged through him—the thrill of the hunt, of the kill.

"Shaking," he whispered to her. "Terrified. Alone. Lost little lamb."

Spike smiled. Then he struck her savagely across the face.

"I love it," he said.

"Buffy!" Angel tried to throw off his guards, but they only held him tighter. He watched helplessly as Spike gripped Buffy's head with one hand and her arm with the other, as he bent her slowly backward, as he leaned in toward her neck.

Buffy was sobbing now. Spike's fangs gleamed in the pale, pale light . . .

Without warning, Xander broke free. Before anyone could stop him, he grabbed his gun and scrambled to his feet, Cordelia and Willow crowding in close behind him.

"Now *that* guy," Willow pointed at Spike, "you can shoot!"

Xander raised the machine gun. He aimed at Spike, tensed, and squeezed the trigger.

Nothing happened.

As Xander stared down at his weapon, he saw that he was holding only a toy—a small plastic gun.

His mouth gaped open. "What the—"

Around the room, Spike's minions were suddenly changing, too—not hideous henchmen any longer, but a very scared assortment of high-school kids and little trick-or-treaters. As Spike gazed at them in slow realization, he suddenly glanced down at his hand.

He was still holding Buffy's wig.

Only Buffy's head wasn't in it.

He glanced up again. Right into Buffy's smiling face.

"Hi, honey," Buffy said. "I'm home."

Spike never had a chance. As all the rage and frustration of her last defenseless hours came flooding through her, Buffy let loose on him with a brutal series of kicks and punches.

Spike sprawled to the ground. Buffy yanked him back to his feet.

"You know what?" she said cheerfully. "It's good to be me."

Again she let loose on him, throwing him viciously into the wall. Spike grabbed an iron bar, trying to fend her off, but Buffy wrenched it away from him. Beating him mercilessly, she stood back and watched as he collapsed once more to the ground.

Spike lay there, stunned. Then, after several seconds, he staggered drunkenly to his feet and took off.

An unsettling peace descended at last, broken only

by the frightened crying of several bewildered children. As Buffy stood there, Xander, Cordelia, and Angel all moved toward her, shocked but alive.

"Hey, Buff," Xander greeted her. "Welcome back."

Buffy smiled at him. "Yeah. You, too."

"You guys remember what happened?" Cordelia regarded them incredulously.

"It was way creepy." Xander frowned. "Like I was there, but I couldn't get out."

Nodding emphatically, Cordelia turned to Angel. "I know the feeling. This outfit is totally skintight."

But she could see that Angel wasn't listening to a word she said. He was totally focused on Buffy.

"You okay?" Angel asked quietly.

Buffy stared back into his eyes—those dark eyes she loved so much—and she could see the worry they still held for her, the unmistakabe relief and concern.

"Yeah," she smiled.

He took her arm and guided her outside, leaving Xander and Cordelia to stare after them.

"Hello?" Cordelia's mouth dropped open in disbelief. "It *felt* like I was talking. My *lips* were moving—"

Xander's advice was glum. "Give it up, Cordy. You're never going to get between those two. Believe me. I know."

Considering this, Cordelia turned back to the dazed little group of trick-or-treaters.

"I guess we should get them back to their parents," she said.

"Yeah. It seems like everybody is—" Xander broke

off, his eyes going anxiously around the room. "Where's Willow?"

He realized suddenly that he hadn't seen her leave. That he hadn't seen her at all, in fact, since he'd snapped out of his spell.

Willow wasn't sure what had happened either. One minute she'd been standing with the others back in the warehouse, but now she was coming back to consciousness on Mrs. Parker's front porch, lying there underneath a sheet.

Groggily, she pushed the costume away. It took a few seconds for her head to clear, to get to her feet and stand up again. She felt alive, at least. Back in her own body and in one piece.

Willow looked down at the sheet and started to throw it over her head.

And then she stopped.

With a boldness that was new to her, she tossed the sheet aside and strode off across the yard.

There was a van stopped at the intersection as Willow started across the street. She held her head high and looked determinedly forward, unaware that Oz was in the driver's seat, watching her every move.

Oz was totally enchanted.

As he watched the confident rocker babe fade out of view from his headlights, a slow smile spread across his face.

"Who *is* that *girl?*" he murmured.

EPILOGUE

Buffy came out of the bathroom. Dressed in comfortable sweatpants and tank top, she looked like herself again as she paused in the doorway of her room. Her face was scrubbed clean; her hair was brushed and shiny, hanging soft about her face.

Her bedroom was dark. The only light glowed in from behind her, gently illuminating the figure on her bed. Angel had been lying there, deep in thought, but now he looked up at her with concern.

"Taa-daa." Buffy struck a pose. "Just little old twentieth-century me."

She crossed the room and sat down next to him. Angel gazed searchingly into her face.

"Are you sure you're okay?" he asked.

"I'll live."

He hesitated a moment. He'd come close to losing

her tonight, and he fought back the urge to pull her into his arms, to never let her go.

"I don't get it, Buffy," he said at last. "Why'd you think I'd like you better dressed that way?"

Buffy's eyes lowered. How could she ever explain to him how important it had seemed to experience that long-ago life Angel had lived, to be a normal young woman, the sort of woman Angel might have loved, to share some secret part of him she'd probably never know.

And yet Buffy realized it had gone even deeper than that. It had also been a longing to understand who Angel truly was, to gain some special insight into the human he once had been. And to bring herself closer—now, *today*—to Angel's heart.

Slowly she raised her eyes again. He was watching her so intently, she felt drawn into the dark depths of his stare.

"I—I just wanted to be a real girl, for once," her voice was barely a whisper. "The kind of fancy girl you liked when you were my age."

For me, Angel thought to himself, *you almost sacrificed yourself for me.*

To Buffy's surprise he laughed softly and shook his head.

"What?" Buffy asked, slightly hurt by his reaction.

"I hated the girls back then," he admitted. "Especially the noblewomen."

Buffy's look was dubious. "You did?"

"They were just incredibly dull. Simpering morons, the lot of them. I always wished I could meet someone . . . exciting."

A soft, lazy smile crept over his lips. He leaned toward Buffy.

"Interesting," he added.

"Really." A warm glow of pleasure spread through her. Her heartbeat began to quicken. "Interesting—like how?"

Angel's smile widened. He knew she was baiting him, and he was all too willing to play along.

"You know how," he scolded her.

He leaned in closer. Their lips were almost touching, and Buffy could feel the faint stirring of his breath against her cheek.

"Still," she sighed innocently, "I've had a hard day, and you should tell me."

"I should," Angel teased.

"Oh, definitely . . ."

And as Angel's lips closed over hers, Buffy surrendered to his long, deep, passionate kiss.

On the morning after Halloween, Giles stood alone inside Ethan's Costume Shop.

It was as if the place had never even existed.

Empty display cases, stripped shelves, overturned mannequins—not a single thing remained anywhere to suggest that a businesss had recently thrived within these walls.

Giles walked slowly around the room, his face pensive. His footsteps echoed ghostly upon the floor.

And then something caught his attention.

There—just across from him—a small rectangular card was propped on a vacant counter.

Giles went over and picked it up.

He stared down at the handwriting, at the three words slashed in bold, black letters.

BE SEEING YOU.

There was no expression on his face now as he finally looked up.

But his eyes were thoughtful—and hard, and cold.

THE SECOND CHRONICLE:

WHAT'S MY LINE?
PARTS 1 AND 2

PROLOGUE

With Halloween over, Buffy tried to resume her life with a fresh sense of purpose.

Once again Sunnydale had been saved from certain tragedy, and in the process she'd discovered that she *much* preferred being herself rather than some helpless female. In the days that followed, she clung to the reassurances Angel had given her—the way he'd touched her that night, the truth in his eyes, the desire in his kisses. She wanted so much to believe that their love could transcend all the obstacles facing them, and that her own life could be just as fulfilling as that of any other young woman her age.

Yet, deep down, Buffy still wasn't convinced.

It was Sunnydale High's Career Fair that brought everything back again, those painful reminders that she was—and always would be—different.

She was sitting with Xander in the lounge that day,

staring glumly down at her test form. Banners hung from the walls, reminding students that Career Fair Starts Tomorrow, and at a table across the room, the school guidance counselor sat sagely behind another sign which read, Vocational Aptitude Tests.

As Buffy lifted her eyes, she saw Willow come in and grab a test, then walk over to join them.

"Are you a people person or do you prefer keeping your own company?" Xander read solemnly from his test. He paused, his brow furrowing. "What if I'm a people person who keeps his own company by default?"

"So, mark 'none of the above,'" Buffy said.

"There *is* no box for none of the above. That would introduce too many variables into their mushroom-head, number-crunching little world."

Willow beamed Xander a smile. "I'm sensing bitterness."

"It's just, these people can't tell from one multiple choice test what we're supposed to do for the rest of our lives," Xander grumbled. "It's ridiculous."

Willow's eyes widened. "I'm kind of curious to find out what sort of career I could have."

"And suck all the spontaneity out of being young and stupid? I'd rather live in the dark."

"We won't be young forever," Willow reminded him.

"I'll always be stupid," Xander shot back. And then, when nobody commented, he added, "Okay, let's not all *rush* to disagree . . ."

The three glanced up at the sound of Cordelia's voice. She was heading straight toward them, test form in hand, flanked by her usual group of Cordelia wannabes.

"'I aspire to help my fellow man,'" she read aloud. "Check."

She stopped, making a decisive mark on her paper. And then she cocked her head and frowned.

"I mean, as long as he's not, like, smelly or dirty or something gross," she clarified.

"Cordelia Chase," Xander sighed, "always ready to offer a helping hand to the rich and pretty."

Cordelia regarded him with a frosty smile. "Which, lucky me, excludes you *twice!*"

She moved off again, her Cordettes tittering as they followed. Xander leveled an impassive stare at her back.

"Is murder *always* a crime?" he asked hopefully.

Buffy glanced down the list of questions in front of her. Then she looked up with a frown.

"Do I like shrubs?"

"That's between you and your God," Xander said.

"What'd you put?" Buffy asked Willow, craning her neck to see.

"I came down on the side of shrubs."

"Go shrubs," Buffy agreed, settling back in her seat. "Okay." Then she put down her pencil, her frown deepening. "I shouldn't even be bothering with this. It's all moot-ville for me. No matter what my aptitude test says—I already know my deal."

"Yep," Xander nodded. "High risk, sub-minimum wage . . ."

Buffy held her pencil in front of him. "Pointy wooden things."

"So why are you even taking the test?" Willow asked.

"It's Principal Snyder's 'hoop' of the week," Buffy said wryly. "He's not happy unless I'm jumping. Believe me, I wouldn't be here otherwise—"

"You're not even a teensy weensy bit curious about what kind of career you could have had?" Willow broke in gently. "I mean, if you weren't already the Slayer and all."

"Do the words *sealed* and *fate* ring any bells for you, Will?" Buffy snapped. "Why go there?"

She stopped, shocked at her outburst. Willow's face looked positively stung.

"You know," Xander informed her, "with that kind of attitude you could have had a bright future as an employee of the DMV."

Buffy nodded, wilting beneath his glare. "I'm sorry. It's just, unless hell freezes over and every vamp in Sunnydale puts in for early retirement, I'd say my future is pretty much a nonissue."

The question of Drusilla's future lay heavily on Spike's mind—it was practically all he could think about these long, tortured nights.

Now, while Drusilla stood at one end of the dining table laying out her beloved Tarot cards, Spike paced anxiously at the other end, a Latin/English dictionary clutched in his hand. He'd instructed Dalton to join them this evening. Of all Spike's followers, Dalton was the one best educated, the one most learned, the only true scholar in the bunch. So as Spike continued to pace, Dalton pored carefully over a large manuscript spread out on the table in front of him.

"Read it again," Spike ordered.

Dalton hesitated, adjusting the spectacles upon his hideous vampire nose. "I'm not sure . . . it could be *Deprimere ille bubula linter.*"

Spike flipped quickly through the dictionary. He stopped at one page, then read slowly, "Debase the beef . . . canoe."

Dalton kept his eyes on the table. Spike slammed him in the head with the book.

"Why does that strike me as *not right?*" Spike demanded.

Drusilla turned to him, humming. In her delicate white gown and black lace shawl, she looked even paler than usual. Swaying softly, she held out her arms to him, opened them wide . . .

"Spike? Come dance."

Instantly Spike bristled. "Give us some peace, would you? Can't you see I'm working?"

The second the words were out, he regretted them. He saw the look on Drusilla's face, the hurt and betrayal in her wide, strange eyes. Her bottom lip quivered, her eyes filled with tears.

"I'm sorry, kitten." Spike went to her, tender now, remorseful. "It's just, this manuscript is supposed to hold your cure. But it reads like jibberish."

Still wounded, Drusilla turned away from him. Spike followed, desperate to appease her.

"I'm frazzed is all," he told her. "I never had the Latin. Even Dalton here, the big brain, even he can't make heads or tails of it."

It was almost too much to bear, seeing her like this, knowing he'd hurt her—and especially in her fragile condition. He looked at her pleadingly, but once more she turned away from him.

"I—I need to change Miss Edith . . ."

And then Spike saw her falter. Suddenly weak, Drusilla tried to grab the table, and Spike rushed to her side.

She was hardly more than a ghost. As Spike gently guided her to a chair, her shawl came loose, revealing dark, ugly bruises along the translucent skin of her arms.

Spike looked away. He could feel the desperation rising inside of him—the utter helplessness so foreign to his nature—and he knelt down at Drusilla's side.

"Forgive me." Spike's voice trembled, dangerously close to tears. "You know I can't stand seeing you like this." And then his voice grew angry with frustration. "And we're running out of time. It's that bloody Slayer. Whenever I turn around she's mucking up the works—"

His voice broke off, leaving only the silence. He quickly bowed his head.

"Shhhhh," Drusilla whispered. Her features softened at his distress; she slipped her fingers beneath his chin and gently lifted his head. "Shhhhhhh . . . you'll make it right. I know."

It was the benediction he'd been hoping for. Gratefully, Spike took her hand and kissed it. And then he stood, fierce once again, and more than ready to take it out on Dalton.

"Well?" Spike demanded. "Come on now. Enlighten me."

Dalton nodded nervously, his fingers skimming over the pages of the manuscript. "I—it looks like Latin, but it's not. I'm not even sure it's a language. Not one I can decipher, anyway—"

"Then *make* it a language!" Spike bellowed, striding over to him. "Isn't that what a transcriber does?"

"Not—not exactly."

Spike grabbed him. He lifted Dalton out of his seat with one hand. Miserably, Dalton braced himself for some serious damage.

"I want the cure," Spike seethed.

At the other end of the table, Drusilla was staring down at her cards again. As Spike prepared to let loose on Dalton, she suddenly stopped him.

"Don't—"

"Why not?" Spike retorted. "Some people find pain"—he slammed Dalton hard in the stomach, doubling him over—"very inspirational."

Before Dalton could recover, Spike grabbed him again.

"He can't help you," Drusilla insisted. "Not without the key."

Spike froze. Very slowly he turned to her.

"The key? You mean the book is in some kind of code?"

Drusilla nodded. Spike dropped Dalton in a messy heap and walked back over to where she was sitting. And then he followed her solemn gaze down to the Tarot card she'd turned.

It was an etching of a ruined crypt. A crypt overgrown with ivy, mouldering majestically above a field of tilted gravestones.

"Is that where we'll find this key?" Spike murmured.

Again Drusilla nodded. A satisfied grin spread slowly across Spike's face.

"I'll send the boys pronto," he said.

Drusilla's eyes widened hopefully. "Now will you dance?"

"I'll dance with you, pet." Spike laughed. "On the Slayer's grave."

He lifted her into his arms. And then, as Dalton watched fearfully, Spike spun his beloved Drusilla around and around the room . . . in time to the music only she could hear.

CHAPTER 1

It was usually quiet in the cemetery, but tonight a storm was threatening.

Buffy walked among the graves, every sense alert to potential danger. This would be the last stop on her patrol tonight, and she was tired, eager to get home. Dead leaves tumbled across the ground, scraping over headstones, riding a stiff wind. And yet suddenly there came a different sound—not the stealthy brewing of thunderclouds, but a closer, more distinct sound—one she'd never heard before.

Buffy stopped, listening. The sound came again—*tink tink tink*—and she frowned, trying to place it. Her eyes wandered slowly over dark tombstones and shadows. And then she noticed something.

The mausoleum stood slightly apart from the other graves, rising high above them in mouldering splendor. Buffy gazed at it for a long time, then finally she began moving toward it.

The sound was louder now. As she neared the front of the mausoleum, she could tell that the noise came from inside, and to her surprise she saw that the solid iron door was standing open. An eerie glow of light flickered across the threshold. Buffy took a deep breath and looked in.

A torch was set in the ground, and it was this light that threw its macabre shadows over the gloomy, rotting interior of the tomb. As Buffy watched, she could see a dark figure pressed close to the far wall, so absorbed in its work that it had no idea she was even there. It seemed to be intent on one of the vault doors, and as the lock finally broke, Buffy saw the thief open the vault and grab something from inside.

Quickly she hurried out again. She positioned herself at the bottom of the mausoleum steps, arms folded casually across her chest as the figure came out.

"Does 'rest in peace' have no sanctity to you people?" Buffy asked in mock surprise. "Oh, I forgot—you're not people."

Dalton froze where he stood. He clutched the red velvet bag in one hand and prepared to defend himself. He didn't think Buffy had heard the second vampire sneaking up behind her. As she pulled out a wooden stake, this new creature lifted its claws and poised for attack.

Buffy wheeled without warning, knocking the vampire back with a vicious, jumping kick. She grabbed him and drove his head into a tree trunk.

The vampire crumpled to the ground. Buffy plunged

the stake into his chest and watched him explode into dust.

"One down," she declared triumphantly, then spun, ready to take on Dalton.

But Dalton wasn't there.

Buffy gazed at the empty steps of the mausoleum.

"One gone," she mumbled, bewildered.

She stood for several minutes, straining her ears through the night. When every instinct told her the danger had gone, she finally headed for home.

Angel was waiting for her. As Buffy started to climb through her window, she could see him inside and so she stopped. Her heart fluttered, sending warmth through her body, the way it always did when she was close to him—when she even *thought* about him.

And this is the way we'll always meet, she suddenly thought—*the only way we can* ever *meet, here in the cover of darkness* . . .

Her heart wrenched in her chest. She froze there on the windowsill and watched.

Angel didn't see her as he moved restlessly among her things, back and forth through her bedroom, picking up one personal item after another, then setting each back down again. He'd never concerned himself much with material possessions; he'd learned early just how cumbersome they could become throughout the centuries. But now, as he inspected childhood toys and private treasures, a whole new picture of Buffy began to emerge. Not just that of a Slayer, a Chosen One, but that of a vibrant young woman, full of life and hopes and dreams and a burning desire to be like other girls her age.

Gingerly, Angel reached out toward a shelf. He ran one finger down the side of a plush pig, and he fought down a sudden ache in his throat.

These were things of a human world.

Things that only reminded him of Buffy's mortality.

Buffy saw him hesitate, saw the muscle tighten in his cheek. Quickly she tossed her equipment bag into the room. As it landed with a thud upon the floor, Angel jumped like he'd been shot. He spun toward her, and Buffy saw with amusement that he was holding her favorite stuffed animal.

"Buffy," Angel sighed in relief. "You scared me."

She swung her legs over the windowsill. "Now you know what it feels like, stealth-guy." She'd meant to be teasing, but that edge had crept back into her voice. "So. Just dropping by for some quality time with Mr. Gordo?"

Angel looked blank. "Excuse me?"

"The pig."

He looked down and realized he still had her plush toy. "Oh, I, no—" Embarrassed, he quickly put it back on the shelf.

"What's up?" Buffy asked casually.

"Nothing."

She tossed him a look. "You don't have 'nothing' face. You have 'something' face. And you don't have to whisper. Mom's in L.A. till Thursday. Art buying or something."

"Then why'd you come in through the window?"

Buffy stared at him. Then she sheepishly glanced back at the window. "Oh. Uh, habit. So what's up?"

The banter fell away. Angel's face grew serious. "I wanted to make sure you were okay. I had a bad feeling."

"Oh, surprise," Buffy said curtly. "Angel comes with bad news."

She could see him watching her in obvious bewilderment, she could read the hurt in his eyes.

"Sorry," she said quietly. "I've been cranky miss all day. It's not you."

"What is it then?"

"Nothing, it's . . . We're having this thing at school—"

"Career week?"

"How'd you know?"

Angel shrugged. "I lurk."

"Oh, right. So you know, then. It's this whole week of 'What's my line?' Only I don't get to play." She hesitated, lowering her eyes. "Sometimes I just want . . ."

She broke off. She gazed hard at the floor.

"You want what?" Angel coaxed her. "It's okay."

"The Cliffs Notes version?" Buffy said seriously. "I want a normal life. Like I had before."

Angel nodded. "Before me."

Silence fell between them. Buffy lifted her head and gazed into the mirror beside her bed. She could see herself so clearly, the weary young woman gazing back with sadness in her eyes.

But she was all alone there in the glass.

Angel had no reflection.

"It's not that," Buffy said carefully. "It's just, this career business has me contemplating the el weirdo that I am. Let's face it—instead of a job I have a *calling.* Okay? No chess club or football games for me. I spend my free time in graveyards and dark alleys—"

"Is that what you want?" Angel broke in. "Football games?"

"Maybe. Maybe not. But you know what?" Buffy could feel the self-pity building inside her, not wanting to feel it, but strangely powerless to stop it. "I'm never going to get the chance to find out. I'm stuck in this deal."

Again that hurt on Angel's face. Buffy felt sick and ashamed.

"I don't want you to feel stuck," Angel told her at last.

"Angel, I don't mean you," Buffy said desperately, trying so hard to explain, wanting him so much to understand. "You're the one freaky thing in my freaky world that makes sense to me." She paused, took a deep breath. "I just get messed sometimes—wish we could be like regular kids."

This time he relented a little. He even managed a halfhearted nod.

"I'll never be a kid," Angel reminded her.

"Okay, then," Buffy conceded, thinking quickly. "Just a regular kid and her two-hundred-year-old, creature-of-the-night boyfriend."

She knew her joke had fallen flat. She watched his eyes travel to the mirror, and then slightly above it, where he seemed to notice something.

"Was this part of your normal life?" Angel asked.

He reached past her, plucking a photograph from the mirror's frame.

It was a younger Buffy, a happier-looking Buffy. She was figure skating and performing a perfect arabesque.

Buffy's face softened as she took the picture from him. "My Dorothy Hamill phase. My room in L.A. was this major shrine—Dorothy posters, Dorothy dolls. I even got the Dorothy haircut." Now it was her turn to feel embarrassed. "Thereby securing a place for myself in the Geek Hall of Fame."

Angel was regarding her with interest. "You wanted to be like her."

"I wanted to *be* her," Buffy corrected him. "My parents used to fight a lot. Skating was an escape. I felt safe . . ."

Her voice trailed away. Angel carefully replaced the photo in the mirror frame.

"When was the last time you put on your skates?" he asked, with an odd gleam in his eyes and a half-smile playing on his face.

Buffy had to think. "Like, a couple hundred demons ago."

"There's a rink out past Route Seventeen." He took a step toward her. "It's closed on Tuesdays."

Buffy looked up at him, scarcely daring to hope. She returned his smile and took a step toward him. "Tomorrow's Tuesday," she said cautiously.

They were close enough to kiss.

"I know."

CHAPTER 2

The outcomes of the aptitude tests had been posted. As students milled about between classes, Xander and Cordelia stood in front of the large sign in the palm court, anxiously reading over the lists, searching for their names.

"Here I am!" Cordelia announced "Personal shopper or motivational speaker. Neato!"

"Motivational speaker?" Xander's look was mildly shocked. "On what? 'Ten steps to a more annoying you'?"

"Oh," Cordelia threw back at him. "And what about you? You're—"

Once again she scanned the lists, this time finding his name. With a burst of laughter, she shook her head and moved off into the crowd, leaving Xander desperately staring at the sign.

"What? What?"

He still couldn't see his name, and Buffy and Willow walked right past him, too deep in girl-talk to stop.

"You and Angel are going skating?" Willow said excitedly. "Alone?"

Buffy nodded. "Unless some unforeseen evil pops up. But I'm in full see-no-evil mode."

"Angel, ice skating . . ."

"I know," Buffy agreed. "Two worlds collide."

They turned as Xander caught up with them. One look at his face told them he was severely disturbed about something.

"Wouldn't you two say you know me about as well as anyone?" Xander demanded. "Maybe even better than I know myself?

"What's this about?" Willow sounded wary.

"When you look at me, do you think prison guard?"

The two girls paused. They looked him over appraisingly.

"Crossing guard, maybe," Buffy said at last. "But prison guard?"

Xander was in full indignation. "They just put up the assignments for the Career Fair. And according to my test results, I can look forward to being gainfully employed in the growing field of corrections."

"At least you'll be on the right side of the bars," Buffy teased.

"Laugh now, missy. They assigned *you* to the booth for Law Enforcement Professionals."

Buffy made a face. "As in police?"

"As in polyester, donuts, and brutality," Xander said.

"Ugh."

Willow's expression brightened. "But . . . donuts . . ."

The mention of food didn't soothe Buffy at all. In fact, she was gazing off in another direction now, where they could see Giles trying to balance a foot-high stack of books under his chin.

"I'll jump off that bridge when I come to it," Buffy said. "First I have to deal with Giles. He's on this Tony Robbins hyper-efficiency kick. He wants me to check in with him now every day after homeroom."

Waving goodbye, she hurried off. Willow turned to Xander.

"You didn't check to see which seminar I was assigned to, did you?" she asked.

"I did," Xander assured her. "And you weren't."

"I wasn't what?"

"On any of the lists."

Willow looked confused. "But I handed in my test. I used a number two pencil."

"Then I guess you must've passed," Xander concluded.

"It's not the kind of test you pass or fail."

"Your name wasn't up there, Will," Xander said again.

He headed off for class, leaving Willow to stare worriedly after him.

The books were just about to fall.

As Giles tried to set them down on the library table, the whole stack tilted and began to topple over, when Buffy suddenly caught them.

"Oh, Buffy." Giles smiled his relief. "Thank you."

Together they eased the stack down safely while Giles continued to talk.

"I've been indexing the Watcher Diaries covering the past two centuries," he told her. "You'd be amazed at how pompous and long-winded some of these Watchers were."

Buffy hid a smile. "Color me stunned."

"I trust last night's patrol was fruitful," Giles went on, opening a notebook.

"Semi. I caught one of two vamps after they stole something from this jumbo mausoleum at the cemetery—"

"They were stealing?" Giles broke in.

"Yep. They had tools and the whole nine yards." Buffy paused, then asked, "What does that mean? The whole nine yards . . . nine yards of what? Now that's gonna bug me all day."

She pondered this a moment longer, then realized Giles was pacing, visibly disturbed.

"Giles, you're in pace mode," Buffy scolded. "What gives?"

"The vampire who escaped, did you see what he took?"

"No, but let me take a wild guess. Some old thing?"

Giles frowned. "I'm serious, Buffy."

"So am I. I bet it was downright crusty."

Giles was definitely not laughing. There was an edge of impatience in his tone.

"So you made no effort to find out what was taken?" he persisted.

Buffy looked up at him, a little surprised by his sharpness.

"Have a cow, Giles. I thought it was just everyday vamp hijinks."

"Well, it wasn't," Giles retorted. "It could be very serious. If you'd made more of an effort to be thorough in your observations—"

"If you don't like the way I'm doing my job," Buffy broke in, hurt, "why don't you find someone else? Oh, right. 'There can be only one.' Long as I'm alive, there *isn't* anyone else. Well, there you go! I don't have to be the Slayer. I could be *dead!*"

Giles regarded her solemnly. "That's not terribly funny. You'll notice I'm not laughing."

"Death wouldn't be much of a change anyway," Buffy rushed right on. "I mean, either way I'm bored, constricted, I never get to shop, and my hair and fingernails continue to grow, so really, what's the dif?"

Giles struggled for composure. "Must we be so introspective *now?*" he asked gently. "Our only concern at this moment should be to discover what was stolen from that mausoleum last night."

The large silver cross lay on a velvet pillow.

Its crossbar appeared to be dotted with holes, yet with no particular pattern or significant design. Instead, the holes seemed to have been randomly placed—very much like Swiss cheese.

"This is it, then?" Spike asked softly.

He sat on the edge of Drusilla's bed, holding out the pillow to her like an offering. Her frail, quivering hands hovered above the cross, and yet she didn't touch it. She looked almost as if she were warming herself.

"It hums," Drusilla murmured. "I can hear it."

Spike smiled delightedly. "Once you're well again, we'll have a coronation down Main Street. We'll invite everyone and drink for seven days and seven nights—"

"What about the Slayer?" Dalton broke in.

He was standing at a respectful distance. Spike whirled around, angry at the interruption.

"She almost blew the whole thing for us," Dalton went on earnestly. "She's trouble."

Spike raised an eyebrow, his voice dripping sarcasm. "You don't say."

The reminder was enough to send him to his feet again, and as he started pacing, his anger quickly grew.

"Trouble?" he echoed mockingly. "She's the gnat in my ear. The gristle in my teeth! The bloody thorn in my *bloody* side!"

He slammed his fist down on the table, alarming even Drusilla.

"Spike—" she whimpered, but Spike immediately cut her off.

"No," he said. "Smart guy is right. We have to do something. There's no way we'll complete your cure with that *bitch* breathing down our necks."

He grew quiet for a moment, thinking.

And then, as realization began to dawn, he slowly nodded his head.

"I need the big guns," he decided. "They'll take care of her. Once and for all."

Dalton looked at him nervously. "Big guns?"

"The Order of Taraka," Spike said.

He was pleased with Dalton's reaction, at the obvious shock and fear.

"The bounty hunters?" Dalton stammered. "For the Slayer?"

Drusilla picked up her Tarot cards.

She peeled three from the deck, and then she gazed at them with a dreamy, faraway smile.

"They're coming to my party," she mumbled. "Three of them."

"But, the Order of Taraka," Dalton rushed on worriedly. "I mean, don't you think that's overkill?"

Spike grinned. He looked down at Drusilla's cards.

"No. I think it's just *enough* kill."

He was pleased with the images he saw there.

Ominous, archetypal etchings that were not quite what they seemed.

A cyclops, a worm, a jaguar.

CHAPTER 3

Career Fair was up and running. By two-thirty that afternoon, Sunnydale students were clustered eagerly around the booths that had been set up in the school lounge. Each booth was manned by representatives from various professions; all of them were there to give advice, offer encouragement, hand out information, and convince students that the real world is fun.

Willow drifted worriedly through the crowds. Her eyes went from one booth to the next—physician, postal worker, policewoman—but she still didn't know where she belonged.

"What are you doing here?" Xander teased, coming up to her. "Fly! Be free, little bird—you defy category!"

"I'm looking for Buffy," Willow told him.

"She left with Giles an hour ago. Some kind of 'field trip' deal."

Willow sighed, "If she doesn't get back soon, Snyder's really—" Without warning she perked up, her whole face brightening. "Done a fantastic job setting up the fair this year, hasn't he, Xander?"

Xander turned to see Principal Snyder right beside them. He immediately began to talk.

"Principal Snyder! Great Career Fair, sir. Really. In fact, I'm so inspired by your leadership, I'm thinking of principal school. I want to walk in your shoes." Xander hesitated, glancing down at the principal's feet. "Not your *actual* shoes, of course. Because you're a tiny person. Not tiny in the small sense, of course . . ." His voice trailed off. He nodded emphatically. "Okay. Done now."

Principal Snyder didn't even grace this with a remark.

"Where is she?" he asked Willow.

Willow looked innocently back at him. "Who?"

"You know who."

"Oh . . ." Willow hesitated, "you mean Buffy? I just saw her—"

"And don't feed me that I-just-saw-her-a-minute-ago-she's-around-here-somewhere story," the principal snapped.

Willow looked like a cornered puppy. "But I did—see her a minute ago. And she is—around here somewhere."

"For what it's worth—" Xander began, but Principal Snyder cut him off.

"It's worth nothing, Harris. Whatever sound comes out of your mouth is a meaningless waste of breath. An airborne toxic event."

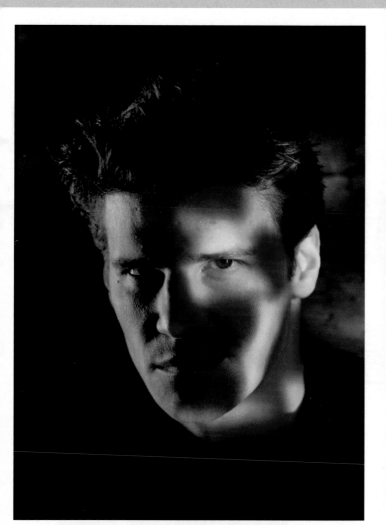

Angel

"This just isn't me."
—Willow

Ripper

"I'll dance with you, pet. On the Slayer's grave. . . ."
—Spike

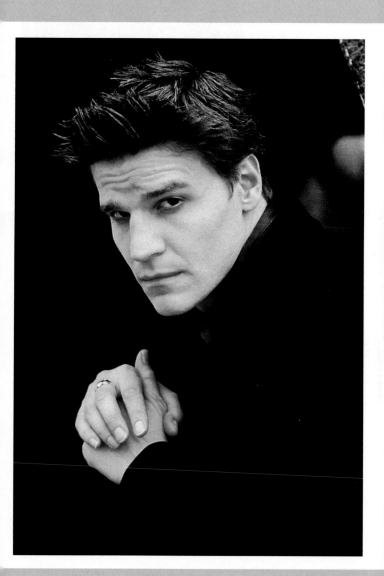

"Did I not see you kissing a vampire?"
—Kendra

"You can attack me, you can send assassins after me . . . that's just fine. But nobody messes with my boyfriend."
—Buffy

Todd MacIntosh helps David get into character.

"I'm glad you feel comfortable enough to be so honest with me," Xander returned amiably. "And I only hope I'm in a position one day to be as honest with you."

The principal gave him a curious look. Almost as though he were studying some rare and dangerous insect.

"Fascinating," he mumbled, and moved off.

"I'd love to stay and chat," Xander turned his attention back to Willow, "but I have an appointment with the warden on standard riot procedure."

"Okay," Willow said. "See you."

She gave a forlorn little wave as he disappeared into the crowd, then jumped as someone came up behind her.

"Willow Rosenberg?" a voice asked.

Willow turned. Two men were standing there, one on either side of her, both wearing identical dark suits and extremely somber expressions. There was an air of supreme authority about them, rather than of danger, yet still Willow shrank back.

"Come with us please?" one of the men said to her now.

Willow's eyes widened. "Excuse me?"

"Let's walk."

Reluctantly she allowed herself to be led past several booths, to a velvet cordon, then up into the elevated section of the lounge, which was now hidden behind a dark curtain. Two freestanding walls separated this area from the general population, and as Willow was led inside, she felt strangely like Alice in Wonderland dropped down the rabbit hole. The space had been refurbished into a deco salon. Soft lighting illuminated the area, while a gentle bossa nova played from hidden speakers. On one wall hung a company logo, and as Willow squinted at it, she realized it very much resembled that of a giant company in the computer industry.

A white-gloved waiter approached her. He held out a silver tray of hors d'ouevres.

"Try the canapé," one of her escorts said. "It's excellent."

But Willow was feeling too overwhelmed to eat just now. "What is all this?"

"You've been selected to meet with Mr. McCarthy, head recruiter for the world's leading software concern," one of the men explained. "The jet was delayed by fog at Sea-Tac, but he should be here any minute." He paused, then added politely, "Please. Make yourself comfortable."

He turned with his partner to leave, but Willow stopped them.

"But I didn't even get my test back," she said.

"The test was irrelevant," the first man replied. "We've been tracking you for some time."

"Is that a good thing?" Willow asked nervously.

"I would think so. We're extremely selective. In fact, only one other Sunnydale student met our criteria."

Before Willow could ask any more questions, both men exited through the partition. In stunned silence she watched them go, then turned around to view her surroundings.

For the first time she realized she wasn't alone in

here. Another student was sitting on the couch, looking completely unfazed by all this strange formality. As Willow took in his thick reddish hair, baggy clothes, and wide, friendly mouth, she recognized him at once as the one she'd gotten tangled up with in the hall on Halloween. But she'd been wearing her ghost costume then, she reminded herself—of course he wouldn't remember her.

She was wrong. As Oz slouched comfortably on the cushions, holding a plate of food, he glanced up to see Willow staring at him. It wasn't often that his face showed emotion. But it certainly did now—with the coolest hint of delight.

After a brief hesitation, Willow moved to the couch and she sat down next to him.

There was a long, awkward silence. Both of them stared straight ahead.

It was Oz who finally spoke. Leaning over with his plate, he offered it to Willow.

"Canapé?"

CHAPTER 4

Giles tried to keep up with Buffy as she hurried through the cemetery. It was clear to him that her feelings were still hurt—she was obviously trying to lose him.

"Buffy," he sighed. "Please. Slow down."

"Get with the program, Giles," Buffy tossed back. "We have work to do, remember?"

"You're behaving in a terribly immature manner—"

"Bingo. Know why? I *am* immature! I'm a teen! I've *yet* to mature!"

Giles struggled for the proper response. "I was simply offering a little constructive criticism—"

"You were harsh," Buffy set him straight. "You act like I *picked* this gig. But I'm the *picked*. Too bad if I want a normal job."

Something must have happened, Giles thought to

himself, wishing like hell he knew what it was. It just wasn't like Buffy to go around feeling sorry for herself like this. He looked around at the sun-dappled headstones and tried to collect his thoughts.

"What you have is more than a . . . gig," he reminded her firmly. "It's a sacred duty."

He recognized the "been there, heard that" look she gave him over her shoulder. He scrambled faster, determined to calm her down.

"Which shouldn't prevent you from eventually procuring a more . . . mundane form of employment if you like," he added. "Such as I have."

"It's one thing being a Watcher and a librarian." Buffy remained stubborn. "They go together—like chicken and . . . another chicken. Two chickens. Or something." Then, noting Giles's look, "You know what I'm saying—*you* can spend all your time with a bunch of books, and no one blinks. But what can I do? Carve stakes for a nursery?"

Giles conceded at last. "Point taken. I suppose I've never really thought about—" He broke off, thought a moment, then brightened. "I say—have you ever considered law enforcement?"

Luckily for Giles they'd reached the mausoleum now, so she didn't even have to come up with a scathing reply.

"This is the place," Buffy said.

She pulled open the heavy iron door and went in, Giles following.

She'd remembered to bring a flashlight with her; now she flicked it on, playing the beam all around the gloomy interior. After a moment, she led Giles over to the vault in the far wall, where the door was still standing open.

"May I?" Giles asked softly.

"Be my guest."

He took the flashlight from her, then shone it into the empty vault.

"It's a reliquary," Giles explained, "used to house items of religious significance. Most commonly, a finger or some other body part from a saint."

"Note to self," Buffy quipped. "Religion—freaky."

Giles turned back around, going over the rest of the wall with the flashlight. Now they could see something else they hadn't noticed before—bold letters carved into the granite above the doorway.

"Du Lac . . ." Giles read the name aloud. Immediately Buffy could hear the recognition in his tone along with unmistakable concern. "Oh dear . . ."

"I hate when you say that," she said flatly.

"Josephus du Lac is buried here."

"Was he a saint?"

"Hardly." Giles frowned. "He belonged to a sect of priests who were excommunicated by the Vatican at the turn of the century."

Buffy raised an eyebrow. "Excommunication *and* sent to Sunnydale. Must have been big with the sinning."

"Remember the book that was stolen from the library by a vampire a few weeks back?" Giles rushed on. "It was written by du Lac and his cohorts—" Frustrated, he broke off, then added, "Damn it. In all the excitement, I let it slip my mind."

"I'm guessing it wasn't a *Taste of the Vatican*

cookbook," Buffy said hopefully, but Giles ignored her.

"The book is said to contain rituals and spells that reap unspeakable evil. However, it was written in archaic Latin, so nobody but the sect members could read it."

Together they walked outside. The sun and fresh air felt good after the dankness of the tomb.

"Then everything's cool," Buffy tried to sound encouraging. "The sect is gone. Worm food like old du Lac, right?"

But Giles looked even more pensive than usual. "I don't like it, Buffy. First the book is taken from the library. Now vampires steal something from du Lac's tomb—"

"You think they've figured out how to read the book?"

"I don't know." Giles shook his head, his eyes deeply troubled. "But something's coming, Buffy. And I guarantee, whatever it is—it's not good."

CHAPTER 5

At the Sunnydale Bus Depot, a bus was just pulling in. It squealed to a stop in a huge cloud of exhaust, and the doors hissed open.

None of the passengers seemed remarkable. Inconspicuous faces in a weary crowd, they stepped off the bus and disappeared just as noneventfully through the doors of the terminal, all bound for ordinary destinations.

Except for one.

This passenger was a veritable giant, standing a good seven feet tall in his enormous boots, and carrying a hard four-hundred pounds on his massive frame.

Greasy hair tangled over his shoulders. A thick, milky cataract covered one eye. His other eye was set deep in fleshy scars and carbuncles he called a face.

His name was Octarus.

And he was on a mission.

A mild-mannered man was striding down the sidewalk on Revello Drive, whistling and carrying a briefcase. He had a round moon-face and a sharply receding hairline, and he wore a suit much too large for his slight build.

His name was Mr. Pfister, and he was also on a mission.

He paused for a moment in front of Buffy's mailbox, reading the name Summers stencilled there.

Then he turned and headed up the walkway of the house next door.

He climbed the stoop and rang the doorbell. He mechanically adjusted the knot in his tie. And when a tired-looking housewife answered the door, he gave her his best salesman's smile.

"Mrs. Kalish?"

"Yes?" the woman answered suspiciously.

"I'm Norman Pfister, with Blush Beautiful Skin Care. I'm not selling anything, so I'm not asking you to buy." He held up his briefcase so she could see. "Just to accept a few free samples."

The woman's suspicions wavered. "Free?"

"Absolutely."

She considered this a moment before letting him in. Mr. Pfister walked past her, and she shut the door behind him.

There was no one else on this quiet street this afternoon.

No one to hear when Mrs. Kalish screamed.

* * *

At the airport, a 767 had just come in for a landing.

As the huge jet engines revved down, the hatch opened to the cargo hold, and a baggage handler climbed inside. He was wearing a Walkman, with heavy metal blasting between his ears. He stopped for an instant and squinted into the dark recesses of the compartment as sunlight blasted in from the opening behind him.

Strange . . .

The young man peered over toward the cargo netting. For a second he could have sworn there'd been a dark silhouette between those crates.

He shrugged. *Probably only shadows* . . .

He busied himself with the luggage, downloading it onto the conveyor belt. He paused long enough to fake the wild motions of a guitar solo, basking in make-believe applause.

And then he thought he saw it again.

Something darting behind that netting, just out of sight.

"What the hell—"

He killed the tape and started toward the shadows.

"Hey!" he called bravely. "You're not supposed to be in here."

No answer. He stopped, his courage faltering.

"Come on—" he started, but never got to finish.

The blows came out of nowhere, rocking him back on his heels. He fell in a heap on the floor, moaning slightly.

From some distant spot through his pain, he thought he heard the echo of footsteps. He thought he saw a shadow fall across him, then step over . . .

Slowly he lifted his eyes.

She was standing there, silhouetted in the doorway, gazing down at him.

A young woman—tall, slim, and exotic-looking—with mocha-colored skin and tight-fitting clothes.

Her forehead was high and wide, her cheekbones finely sculpted; her long black hair had been knotted at the back of her head, where it hung down her back in a thick ponytail. But it was her eyes which struck fear into the young man now—for even though he tried to look away from them, her stare seemed to hold him.

Her eyes were large and black, curiously almond-shaped. They were at the same time feline, feral, and altogether ruthless.

The eyes of a hunter. The eyes of a predator.

To the young man's relief, she suddenly turned and jumped down onto the tarmac.

Her name was Kendra.

And there was much she had to do.

CHAPTER 6

School had been over for hours.

As soon as Buffy and Giles had returned from the cemetery, they'd called Xander and Willow to an emergency conference, and the four of them had been gathered in the library ever since, discussing the du Lac tomb.

"So Giles is sure that the vampire who stole his book is connected to the one you slayed last night?" Willow asked Buffy. "Or is it 'slew'?" she frowned.

"Both are correct," Giles said absentmindedly as he paced among bookshelves. At last he emerged from the stacks with a yellowed periodical. "And yes. I'm sure."

He set the magazine down before them. They could see now that it was a *National Geographic,* published in 1921.

"Du Lac was both a theologian and a mathematician," Giles explained. "This article described an invention of his, which he called the du Lac Cross—"

"Why go to all the trouble of inventing something and then give it a weak name like that?" Xander interrupted. "I'd have gone with 'Cross-o-matic!' or 'The Amazing Mr. Cross!' . . ."

He broke off as they all stared at him. Giles, ignoring Xander, opened the magazine, indicating a discolored photograph of the cross, while Willow began to peruse the accompanying article.

"The cross was more than a symbol," Giles went on. "It was also used to understand certain mystical texts, to decipher hidden meanings and so forth."

Buffy looked up at him, frowning. "You're saying these vampires went to all that trouble for your basic decoder ring?"

Giles regarded her blankly. And then he said, "Actually, I guess I am."

"According to this," Willow said, still intent on the article, "du Lac destroyed every one of the crosses, except the one buried with him."

Again Buffy frowned. "Why destroy his own work?"

"I suppose he feared what might happen if the cross fell into the wrong hands," Giles replied.

"A fear we'll soon get to experience for ourselves, up close and personal," Xander reminded them.

"Unless," Giles murmured, "we preempt their plans."

Willow leaned forward onto the table "How?"

"By learning what was in the book before they do." Giles paused, regarding them with grim purpose.

"Which means we can expect to be here late to-night—"

Willow beamed. "Goody! A research party!"

"Will," Xander admonished her, "you need a life in the worst way—"

"Speaking of," Buffy broke in cheerily, "I have to bail. I promise I'll be back bright and early, perky and ready to slay."

The look Giles gave her was perplexed. "This is a matter of some urgency, Buffy."

"I know," she said quickly. "But you have to admit, I lack in the book area. You guys are the brains. I'd just be around for moral support—"

"That's not true, Buffy," Xander deadpanned. "You totally contribute. You go for snacks."

Buffy glanced at Willow. Girl-thoughts and secrets flew between them.

"She *should* go," Willow agreed. "You know, gather her strength."

Giles considered this a moment. "Perhaps you're right. There may be fierce battles ahead."

"But Ho Ho's are a vital part of my cognitive process," Xander argued.

Buffy gave him a look. "Sorry, Xand. I have some-thing I really need to do tonight."

She hurried out of the room, leaving Giles and Xander totally bewildered.

The ice-skating rink looked beautiful tonight.

Like some magical place, Buffy thought, and she smiled to herself.

She was completely alone, and as she skated round

and round on the ice, moonlight filtered in from the high windows, bathing her in a soft silvery glow.

Buffy breathed deeply of the cool air. She came to a stop, savoring her freedom, then took off again, picking up speed. She'd been afraid she wouldn't remember how to skate, but now she realized she shouldn't have worried. Every technique came easily back to her. She moved gracefully, effortlessly, her hair blowing gently around her face.

So intent was she on her happiness, that she didn't even feel the eyes watching her from the bleachers. Didn't even notice the cruel, scarred face that marked her every movement from the dark.

Octarus looked down at her with an evil grin. He watched as she spun into a tight pirouette and then sailed off again to the far end of the rink.

Buffy *felt* magical tonight. Completely transported, her heart soared with joy—something she hadn't felt for such a long, long time. She pivoted now, skating backward, growing braver, going faster. She launched into an airborne twist, but felt her balance suddenly shift at the apex. Landing hard, the momentum carried her across the ice a good ten feet before she finally slid to a stop.

Buffy caught her breath. She saw a shadow move across the ice in front of her, and she immediately looked around.

"Angel?"

Giant hands clamped about her neck. Octarus lifted her like a rag doll and carried her off the ice to the rink's rubber deck, ruthlessly pinning her to the wall.

Buffy had no idea what was happening. Caught completely off guard, she thrashed and fought and wrenched at his monstrous hands. She couldn't break his grip. She could only feel it closing, tighter and tighter around her throat, and she realized suddenly that she was going to die.

Buffy struggled harder than ever. Her face was a mask of terror. Everything was going black . . .

"Buffy!" a voice shouted.

As Octarus whipped around, Angel's fist slammed into his face. Octarus lost his grip on Buffy, and she fell to the floor, gasping for breath.

But Angel's rage was uncontrollable now. Buffy could see that his handsome face had changed into that of a vampire, and Octarus smashed a ham-sized fist straight into it. Angel went sprawling across the ice. Jumping up again, he quickly realized he was trapped in an alcove. He gave a furious roar and bravely stood his ground, even as Octarus moved in for the kill.

Buffy sprang to her feet in an instant. She vaulted over a wooden bench and landed directly behind Octarus. As he turned around, she took to the air with a spinning wheel kick, leading with the glistening blade of her ice skate.

She saw the silvery flash across his throat.

She heard the sickening rip of flesh.

Even Angel grimaced as Octarus clutched his gaping wound. The giant gazed down at Buffy in both shock and betrayal, and then lumbered toward her once again.

Buffy moved out of his way. He staggered past her,

out onto the ice, somehow pathetic now in his determination.

Buffy watched in grim silence. She felt Angel come up behind her, felt the pressure of his body as he leaned against her.

And then Octarus collapsed.

Without a word, he dropped heavily to his knees and fell facedown on the ice.

"He's passing under our feet," Drusilla murmured dreamily. "Right now."

She gazed down at the Cyclops card in front of her. With thin, pale fingers, she turned it over, then looked up at Spike.

"No worries," Spike assured her, trying to hide his concern. "We're close to decoding the manuscript. We just need a little more time."

Of course, he wasn't fooling her. No one knew him like Drusilla did, and now she lay a cold hand gently upon his brow.

"Time is ours," she whispered, stroking his cheek, smoothing away the worry. "It brings the Slayer closer to *them.*"

Together they stared at the remaining Tarot cards. The Worm and the Jaguar.

CHAPTER 7

Angel knelt cautiously beside the fallen giant.

His anger hadn't completely cooled yet, and there was a bad cut above one of his glowing vampire eyes. He heard Buffy limp up painfully behind him.

"And the Hellmouth presents 'Dead Guys on Ice'," she quipped. "Not exactly the evening we were aiming for."

Angel scarcely heard her. He was too busy staring down at the ring on Octarus's finger. Lifting the massive hand, he studied the glyphlike pattern etched there on the ring's surface.

"You're in danger," Angel said tightly. "You know what the ring means?"

Buffy thought a moment. "I just killed a Superbowl champ?"

"I'm serious. You should go home and wait until you hear from me."

Angel let Octarus's hand drop back down onto the ice. He turned around to Buffy, suddenly noticing her pain.

"Are you okay?"

"What about you?" Buffy countered. "That cut—"

"Forget about me. You're hurt."

He could see right through her—the defiant posture, the quick smile. She was definitely shaken, but still putting on her brave face.

"Hey. No biggy," she assured him. "I've been slammed by bigger sides of beef than that."

"No, you haven't."

At that, Buffy faltered. "No," she agreed. "I haven't."

"This is bad, Buffy," Angel said solemnly. "We have to get you someplace safe."

He saw the quick flash of alarm in her eyes. "You mean—hide?"

"Let's just get you out of here."

He started to move, but Buffy stopped him, staring up at the cut on his brow.

"Wait. Your eye is all . . . Let me—"

She reached up to wipe off the blood.

Angel backed away, lowering his head.

"Come on," Buffy scolded gently. "Don't be a baby. I won't hurt you."

She tried to coax him closer, but Angel only shook his head. "It's not that," he mumbled. "I—you shouldn't have to touch me when I'm like this."

Buffy was at a loss. "Like what?"

He was half turned away from her. She had to strain to hear his voice.

"You know. When I'm . . ."

"Oh," Buffy said.

She stared at him for a long, long time. She felt her heart ache deep within her—a rush of love and pity and understanding.

Slowly, deliberately, she drew off her gloves and placed her hands upon his vampire face. Humiliated, Angel looked away, yet strangely enough, couldn't seem to pull back. It was almost as if the gentleness of Buffy's touch held him there in place, though every instinct told him to run.

Buffy turned his face back to hers. Tenderly she ran her bare fingers along his hideous features, gazing deep into his eyes.

"I didn't even notice," she whispered.

No one had ever touched him like this. Touched the shadow within him, touched the dark thing he'd become all those many years ago. Angel felt overwhelmed with emotions, feelings he'd long forgotten, feelings he never believed he could ever have again.

Buffy drew him closer. Their eyes held, their lips met . . .

Buffy melted into his kiss. And for just this one brief moment they were ordinary lovers, ordinary people, safe and happy in each other's arms.

Safe and happy while Kendra watched them.

From her hiding place in the shadows, she watched them and made her plans.

CHAPTER 8

The first thing Buffy did the next morning was take the ring to Giles.

He'd been studying it closely for some time now, comparing it to an etching he'd found in a book. Xander and Willow were at the table, and Buffy sat nearby with an ice pack on her knee, trying not to think about last night's misadventure. She still felt shaky, and she definitely looked the worse for wear. If Angel hadn't been there to battle Octarus, Buffy knew she might very well not have survived.

"This guy was hard core, Giles," she couldn't help saying for the tenth time. "And Angel was power-freaked by the ring."

Giles gave a slight nod. "I'm afraid he was not overreacting. The ring is worn only by members of the Order of Taraka. They are a society of demon assassins dating back to King Solomon—"

"And didn't they beat the Elks last year in the Sunnydale Adult Bowling League Championship?" Xander asked seriously.

Giles ignored him. "Their credo is to sow discord and kill the unwary."

"Bowling is a vicious game—"

"That's enough, Xander!" Giles said sharply.

The three friends glanced at each other. It was a tone Giles seldom used with any of them, and when he did, Buffy knew to worry.

"I'm sorry," Giles relented, "but this is not time for jokes. I need to think."

"These assassins," Buffy asked him, "why would they be after me?"

"'Cause you're the scourge of the underworld?" Willow piped up.

Buffy made a face. "Yeah, but I haven't been that scourgy lately."

"I don't know," Giles admitted. "But I think the best thing to do is to find a secure location. Someplace out of the way where you can go until we decide on the best course of action—"

That did it. Buffy stumbled to her feet, officially freaked.

"Okay." She held up her hands. "You and Angel have both told me to head for the hills. What's the deal?"

"I—this is an extraordinary circumstance," Giles stammered.

"You're saying I can't handle this?" Her voice sounded frightened. "These guys are that bad?"

"You might—they're . . ." Giles pressed a hand to his forehead, collecting himself. "They're a breed apart, Buffy. Unlike vampires they have no earthly desire except to collect their bounty. To find their target and *eliminate* it."

Buffy felt like she was having an out-of-body experience. She could hear Giles's voice, yet it sounded faint and faraway. She forced herself to pay careful attention.

"And you are the target," Giles was continuing. "You can kill as many of them as you like. It won't make any difference, because where there is one, there will be another. And another. They won't stop coming until the job is done."

He paused, fixing her with a worried look.

"The worse of it is, they are *masters* of deceit. Vampires are bound by the night, but these predators can be anywhere, any time. They can appear as normal as the next person. Just another face in the crowd."

Buffy gazed back at him, feeling cold. She could sense the deep fear beneath his logic.

"You might not ever know when one of them is near," Giles finished quietly. "Not until the moment of your death."

In the house next door to Buffy's, Mr. Pfister was whistling to himself.

He'd pulled up his chair in front of a second-story window, and he was looking through binoculars directly into Buffy's bedroom.

Mrs. Kalish—or at least what was left of her—was lying on the floor.

Now she was little more than a desiccated corpse. Worms crawled out of her nose and mouth, squirming their way across the floor to where Mr. Pfister kept watch.

He sat very calmly as the worms wriggled up his leg and around his waist, as they reached his right arm, which was only partially formed up to the wrist.

The nub of his arm seemed to be moving.

The nub of his arm seemed to be throbbing, undulating, as the teeming mass of slimy worms regrouped themselves, becoming his hand.

Delicately, Mr. Pfister picked up a steaming cup of tea.

He sipped.

And he waited.

Buffy left the library, feeling even more shaken and vulnerable than before.

The halls were packed with people. As she shouldered her way through the Career Fair crowds, she tried to ignore the pain in her knee and keep herself in full alert-mode.

"They can appear as normal as the next person . . . just another face in the crowd."

She tried to shut out Giles's words as they echoed over and over in her head. Her whole body felt like a spring wound too tight. Her eyes darted warily back and forth, side to side, and everyone who passed her seemed a potential threat.

These are people I know, Buffy tried arguing with

herself. *I see them practically every day, all of them are innocent.*

But were they really?

The chaos around her began melting into a dull roar.

She moved cautiously past lockers, past mobbed tables and booths, past classmates and friends, past a policewoman chatting with students, past a pair of Cordettes minus their leader Cordelia . . .

Without warning a guy in the crowd came toward her.

In Buffy's paranoid state, he seemed to actually *lunge* toward her—and he was coming way too fast.

Something's not right!

Instantly she reached out, grabbing the guy by the collar. She shoved him fiercely into a wall.

"Try it!" she shouted.

Oz knew better than to struggle. This girl was stronger than most guys he'd ever known.

So instead he just looked quizzically into Buffy's face.

"Try what?" he asked.

She stared at him. She swallowed. And then she let him go.

"Sorry," she mumbled.

"I'm still not clear on what I'm supposed to try," Oz said again, cautiously.

Buffy looked around. People were staring, and her face flushed hot with embarrassment.

"Nothing," she muttered.

She headed for the door. She threw it open and bolted outside.

Oz stared after her thoughtfully.

"A tense person," he decided.

"I wish there was more we could do," Willow sighed.

She looked down at the table, at the volumes and volumes of books she and Giles had tenaciously been searching since that morning. But now it was night, and she was feeling more than a little discouraged.

Giles looked up at her, his own face mirroring her fatigue and concern.

"We're doing all we can," he assured her. "The only course of action is to decipher the contents of the stolen book."

"I've never seen Buffy like that," Willow broke in worriedly. "She just took off . . ."

"She didn't go home," Xander announced. They turned as he entered the library, a gloomy look on his face. "I let the phone ring a few hundred times before I remembered her mom's out of town."

"Maybe Buffy unplugged the phone," Giles suggested, but Xander shook his head.

"It's a statistical impossibility for a sixteen-year-old girl to unplug a telephone."

They both looked at Willow. She nodded in silent confirmation.

Giles began to pace. "Perhaps my words of caution were a bit too alarming—"

"You *think?*" Xander threw back at him, and Willow hurried to referee.

"It's good that she took you seriously, Giles," she assured him. "I just wish we knew where she was."

Buffy had been walking for hours.

Tired and cold, she turned onto her own street and continued limping along the sidewalk till she came to her house. All the windows were dark. The shadows around her were still.

She knew she wouldn't feel safe here.

No place would feel safe tonight.

She lowered her head and kept walking. Her shoulders hunched against the chilly breeze, and her heart began that old, familiar aching deep inside—that yearning to be normal, to have a normal life.

She didn't realize where she was going, not until she stopped and found herself in front of Angel's basement dwelling.

She stood there staring at his door, and then finally she knocked.

"Angel?"

No answer.

She tried the door, but found it locked.

Forcing the lock, Buffy went in. The place was quiet and dark, the only light spilling in faintly from the hallway behind her.

"Hey . . ." she called softly.

She clicked on a lamp and looked around.

Not overly decorated, but comfortable, she decided. A desk, a chair, a table, a tall folding screen, a dresser, heavy curtains. There were exotic statues in glass cases. There was an unmade bed.

Buffy walked to the bed and sat down. Cautiously she flexed her tender knee, then began to massage it.

Her exhaustion was catching up with her now. Her exhaustion . . . and her fear.

Fighting back tears, she curled up in Angel's bed. Small and alone she lay there on top of his covers, breathing in the scent of him from his pillow.

It was a long time before Buffy finally shut her eyes. And then, at last, she slept.

CHAPTER 9

The Alibi Room was probably the seediest bar in Sunnydale.

As a rule lights were kept low here—to hide both the decor *and* the patrons—and the bartender was a shifty-eyed bottom-dweller named Willy. He prided himself on being a small-time hustler, but he was even prouder of the fact that he moved in the underworld of vampires.

Tonight Willy was cleaning up, giving the floor a perfunctory once-over with his broom. It was after-hours and he wasn't expecting anyone, so when the shadowy figure appeared in the doorway, he got annoyed.

"We're closed," Willy scowled. "Can't you read the sign?"

The figure moved slowly into the room.

As Willy looked up and recognized Angel, his whole

demeanor changed. He'd always been scared of Angel—he didn't want any trouble.

"Oh," he laughed nervously, "hey, Angel. I didn't recognize you in the dark there."

Angel didn't answer. He simply stood and stared.

"What—what can I do for you tonight?" Willy chatted, already putting distance between them. He busied himself near the bar, trying to sound casual.

"I need some information," Angel said.

"Yeah?" Again that nervous laugh. "Man. That's too bad. 'Cause I'm staying away from that whole scene. I'm living right, Angel."

Angel's voice was smooth as silk. "Sure you are, Willy. And I'm taking up sunbathing."

"Come on now," Willy's voice cracked. He swallowed hard, trying to force down his growing fear. "Don't be that way. I treat you vamps good. I don't hassle you. You don't hassle me. We all enjoy the patronage of this establishment. Everybody's happy."

But Angel was coming toward him. He was walking over to Willy with slow, measured steps, and Willy could feel danger closing in around him.

"Who sent them?" Angel asked.

Willy's nerves were about to explode. "Who sent who?"

Lightning fast, Angel's hand clamped around Willy's neck. The broom clattered to the floor as Willy gasped for breath.

"The Order of Taraka," Angel said calmly.

"I tell you"—Willy's eyes bulged with panic—"I haven't been in the loop."

"Let's try again. The Order of Taraka. They're after the Slayer."

"Come on, man . . ." Willy whimpered.

"Is it Spike?"

Angel tightened his grip. He lifted Willy off the floor. Willy tried desperately to choke out a negotiation.

"Angel, hey . . . I—I got some fresh pig's blood in. Good stuff. My fence said the white cell count is—"

His words gurgled in his throat. It suddenly dawned on him that Angel was only moments away from squeezing the life out of him.

"You know," Angel mused, "I'm a little rusty when it comes to killing humans. It could take *a while.*"

"Spike will draw and quarter me, man!"

At this, Angel relaxed his grip. He set Willy back on his own two feet.

"I'll take care of Spike," Angel said.

"You *know* he ordered those guys," Willy broke at last, words tumbling out in a rush. "Spike's sick of your girl getting in his way."

"Where can I find him?"

"I tell you that, and I'm gonna need relocating expenses," Willy whined. "It'll cost you—"

Angel slammed his head into the counter, sending glasses, plates, pieces of food and other debris scattering across the bar and onto the floor. Angel's fingers tightened around his neck.

"It will cost *who?*" Angel prompted him

"Okay . . . Okay!" Willy gasped. "He and that freaky chick of his are—"

Angel squeezed tighter. He was so intent on Willy's information that he never saw the broom handle flying toward his head. Before he even realized what was happening, Angel was blind-sided across the temple. He hit the floor hard, and Willy fell in a heap at his side.

Dazed, Angel looked up. He could see a tall, exotic woman standing over him, wearing a large medallion around her neck. Her whole stance, her whole attitude radiated lethal power. She had a strange foreign accent, and her voice rang with utter contempt.

"Where is she?" Kendra demanded.

Angel kept staring. He shook his head and spit blood onto the floor.

"The girl," Kendra said. "Where *is* she?"

There was no doubt in Angel's mind as to who she was talking about. He answered her with calm defiance.

"Even if I knew, I wouldn't tell you."

Kendra broke the broom handle over her knee. "Then die."

Instantly, Angel rolled out of the way. He felt a sudden swish of air as the makeshift stake plunged down toward his heart. He jumped to his feet, but Kendra was on him again in a flash. Willy raced for the exit and disappeared.

There was no holding back now. As Angel and Kendra fought savagely, they moved through the main room of the club, battling their way toward the rear. The bar's storage area was basically a floor-to-ceiling metal cage where expensive liquor was locked away, and as the two of them crashed inside, bottles shattered everywhere.

Kendra glared at Angel's face. He'd transformed into a vampire now, and his eyes were full of rage. He took up a broken bottle, thrusting it at her to fend her off, and for a split second Kendra hesitated.

"Who are you?" Angel growled.

Kendra backed out of the storage area. Her eyes were wary and she was breathing hard, yet there was an unnerving coolness about her.

"I won't hurt you," Angel promised, "if you tell me what I need to know."

And then, unexpectedly, she smiled.

Angel was incredulous.

"You think this is funny?" he demanded.

Without warning, the door of the storage cage slammed shut.

He watched in disbelief as Kendra bolted it.

"I think it's funny *now,*" she mocked him.

Angel leapt to the door, shaking it viciously, trying to break the lock.

"That girl," Kendra said. "The one I saw you with before—"

"You stay away from her!"

"I'm afraid you are not in a position to threaten."

Angel pressed his face to the metal gate. "When I get out of here I'll do more than threaten—"

"Then I suggest you move quickly," Kendra replied, glancing at a row of high windows that ran along one wall of the storage cage. Uneasily, Angel followed her eyes.

"Eastern exposure," Kendra explained. "The sun comes in a few hours." A smile touched her lips. "More than enough time for me to find your girlfriend."

Frustrated, Angel watched her go.

He threw himself desperately against the door of the cage—and then again and again.

But the lock held fast.

And night crept steadily on toward morning.

CHAPTER 10

Giles wasn't sure what time it was.

He only knew that it was somewhere in the wee hours of the morning, and that he hadn't left the library since yesterday.

Bleary-eyed and rumpled, he talked on the telephone now while riffling through yet another book.

"Xander? No, I still haven't heard from Buffy. I think you should go to her house and check on her . . ."

His voice trailed away as he noticed something on one of the pages.

Something important.

"Right away," Giles replied as Xander rattled on. "I don't know . . . get Cordelia to drive you."

He hung up. Quickly he moved over to the table where Willow had fallen asleep at the computer.

Giles shook her gently. Willow woke with a start, her voice shrill as she cried out.

"Don't warn the tadpoles!"

Giles stared down at her, startled by her outburst.

"My goodness," he frowned. "Are you all right?"

"Giles? What are you doing here?"

"You're in the library, Willow. You fell asleep."

"Oh . . . I . . ."

"'Don't warn the tadpoles'?" Giles lifted an eyebrow, and Willow's expression turned sheepish.

"I—I have frog fear." Seeing the amusement on Giles's face, she added, "I'm sorry . . . I conked out."

"Please," Giles reassured her. "You've gone quite beyond the call of duty. And, fortunately, I think I've finally found something."

"You did?"

He nodded, holding up his book. "I had to go back to the Lutheran Index. But I found a description of the missing du Lac manuscript. It's a ritual, Willow. I haven't managed to decipher the exact details, but I believe the purpose is to restore a weak and sickly vampire to full health."

Willow's eyes widened. "A vampire like Drusilla?"

"Exactly."

"What does that have to do with the Order of Taraka? The assassins?"

"I would imagine Spike called them here to get Buffy out of the way," Giles replied. "I'm sure he wants nothing to come between him and his plans to revive his lady love."

Willow looked pleased. "So this is good. We know what the deal is."

"I wish I could agree," Giles sighed. "But all we know is the goal of the ritual. We don't know where it will take place or when . . . we don't know what it entails—"

Willow's face fell. "So this is bad."

"No. No. We just have more work to do."

He tried to smile encouragingly, but Willow gave him a strange look.

"Then why are you all pinched?" she asked tentatively.

Giles stared at her, more worried than ever.

"By George, I think he's got it."

Smiling triumphantly, Spike watched as Dalton closed the du Lac manuscript. With the transcription complete at last, he took the sheet of paper and swept over to Drusilla.

"The key to your cure, ducks!" Spike announced.

He gazed at her adoringly—the pale, consumptive wraith that was Drusilla. She was propped up on a velvet couch, her Tarot cards laid out on her lap, and Spike pressed close to her.

"The missing bloody link!" he went on. "It was—"

"Right in front of us," Drusilla added.

Weakly she took his hand. She led it to one of the cards.

The image Spike saw there was of an angel. But an angel that was falling, plummeting through the sky to an all but certain doom.

Drusilla raised her strange, dark eyes.

"The whole time," she finished.

CHAPTER 11

The neighborhood was just beginning to waken.

It was still very early, but Xander and Cordelia were already parked in front of Buffy's house, making their way up to her porch.

"I can't even believe you." Cordelia's shrill voice shattered the morning's tranquility. "You drag me out of bed this early for a ride? What am I, mass transportation?"

Xander knocked loudly on the front door. "That's what a lot of the guys say. But it's just locker-room talk. I never pay it any mind."

"Great. So now I'm your taxi *and* your punching bag."

"I like to think of you more as my witless foil, but have it your way." The door was locked, so Xander began trying windows, searching for a way in. "Come on, Cordy. You can't be a member of the Scooby

Gang if you aren't willing to be inconvenienced now and then."

He found what he was looking for. Unlatching the window, he climbed inside.

"Oh, right," Cordelia rolled her eyes. " 'Cause I lie awake at night hoping you tweekos will be my best friends. And that my first husband will be a balding, demented, homeless man—"

She broke off as Xander opened the door.

"Buffy could be in trouble," Xander said seriously.

"And, what, exactly, are you going to do about it if she is?" Cordelia asked. They were standing in the living room, and Cordelia scanned the furnishings with a practiced eye. "If you hadn't noticed—you're the lameness. *She's* the superchick or whatever."

"At least I'm lameness that cares. Which is more than you can say." Xander wasn't kidding now. He turned away from her and headed in the other direction. "I'm going to check upstairs."

Pouting, Cordelia stayed behind. She started to take another quick inventory of Buffy's living room when she was startled by a knock on the front door.

Looking out the window at the top of the door, Cordelia saw a bland, balding salesman, who tipped his hat and held up a briefcase for her to see.

Blush Beautiful Skin Care.

That was enough for Cordelia. She opened the door at once.

"Good day," he said politely. "I am Norman Pfister with Blush Beautiful Skin Care and Cosmetics. I was wondering if I might interest you in some free samples?"

"Free?"

Cordelia hesitated. This wasn't even her house, but the offer was just too tempting to resist.

She stepped aside so Mr. Pfister could come in.

And then she closed the door.

In the back storage area of the bar, the first glow of morning light was just beginning to warm the windows.

In human form once again, Angel could feel the dangerous prickling along his skin, could feel the faint throb of panic rising inside him.

Desperately he tried to tear the metal door from its hinges.

He was running out of time.

Angel's apartment was a cool, dark tomb.

A haven from the waking world.

Buffy still lay in Angel's bed, her body curled among his blankets, her arms wrapped tightly around his pillow.

A smile touched her lips.

Now, for the moment, she was safe . . .

Safe and loved in Angel's phantom embrace.

But there was that *sound*.

That strange, disturbing sound as of something moving about in the apartment. A soft, stealthy sound, yet loud enough to rouse Buffy at last from her wonderful dream.

Her eyelids fluttered open.

As the axe slammed into her pillow, only inches from her neck, Buffy twisted herself away.

She leapt nimbly from the bed. From somewhere far back in her brain came the sudden realization that the second assassin had found her, and she stared defiantly into the woman's exotic eyes.

"You must be number two," Buffy challenged her, but Kendra again swung the axe.

Buffy dodged the razor-sharp blade. Kendra refused to give up.

"Thanks for the wake-up," Buffy taunted. "But I'll stick with my clock radio."

For the third time the axe started to come down—only Buffy caught Kendra's arm in midflight. To Buffy's distress, she couldn't seem to wrench the axe away—Kendra's strength was every bit as powerful as her own. The two of them were locked in a dead-even struggle, like an arm wrestling match between perfect twins. For a split second they met each other's eyes and felt an uncanny twinge of recognition.

Then Buffy took advantage of the moment. Kicking out, she sent the axe flying across the room. She swept Kendra's legs out from under her and watched as her opponent hit the floor.

But Buffy didn't expect Kendra to recover so quickly. To her surprise she felt her own legs being pinned, and in the next instant Buffy landed on the floor beside her.

Now the two of them wrestled furiously, rolling about on the floor. Kendra's blows were precise and well-aimed, but Buffy managed to elude them, one minute fighting on top of Kendra, the next minute struggling beneath her. Angel's apartment was in shambles. They smashed into his table, his bookshelf, his dresser . . .

Buffy was getting fed up.

"Come on," she warned Kendra. "Don't make me do the chick fight thing."

For a second, that seemed to confuse Kendra. Panting for breath, she gasped out, "Chick . . . fight?"

"You know—"

Buffy dug her fingernails into Kendra's hand. As Kendra cried out, Buffy jerked her violently by the hair and threw her off balance. *Chick fight,* she thought to herself. *Have I sunk so low?*

"Clichéd," Buffy said aloud, "but effective."

But now both of them were on their feet again. They circled like animals, both gasping for breath.

Buffy steeled herself. She was ready for the final offensive. She glared furiously into Kendra's eyes and prepared to spring.

"Who are you?" Kendra suddenly asked.

Buffy froze. She stared in disbelief at the strange young woman.

"What do you mean who am I? You *attacked* me. Who the hell are *you?"*

Kendra glared back at Buffy. Proud and defiant to the very end.

"I am Kendra," she said. "The Vampire Slayer."

CHAPTER 12

Buffy stared.

Kendra stared back.

The two of them continued to circle each other, fists raised and ready. For a long moment there was only the ragged sound of their breathing.

"Let's start again," Buffy said at last. "You're the *who?*"

"I'm the Slayer," Kendra replied.

Buffy was speechless. The young woman across from her radiated poise and intensity. There was a faintly regal air about her. And it was way obvious she didn't take anything from anybody.

Still, the whole thing was totally ridiculous.

"Nice cover story," Buffy told her. "Here's a tip— try it on someone who's not the *real* Slayer."

"You can't stop me," Kendra returned. "Even if

you kill me, another Slayer will be sent to take my place."

Buffy was running out of patience. "Could you stop with the Slayer thing? *I'm* the damn Slayer!"

"Nonsense. There is but one—and I am she."

Again Buffy lapsed into silence, totally baffled by this turn of events. Kendra was so annoyingly earnest, she couldn't help but wonder . . .

"Okay," Buffy relented, almost reluctantly. "Scenario: I back off. You back off. You promise not to go all wiggy until we go to my Watcher and figure out what this is all about."

Kendra frowned. "Wiggy?"

"You know—no kicko, no fighto?"

Kendra paused, considering. Then she stood back, folding her arms across her chest. "I accept your scenario."

They still didn't trust each other. With suspicion and more than a little contempt in their eyes, they let down their guard at last, but each continued to silently assess the other.

At last Kendra said, "Your English is very odd, you know."

"Yeah, it's something about being woken by an *axe*. Makes me talk all crazy." Buffy paused, then added, "So you were sent here?"

"Yes, by my Watcher."

"To do what, exactly?"

"To do my duty," Kendra informed her. "I am here to kill vampires."

* * *

Angel looked up at the window high on the wall of the storage area.

Sun was streaming through the barred glass, spilling light into the room.

He could hardly breathe now.

Buffy . . .

Huddled in a corner, he tried to draw into himself, tried to put even an inch more distance between himself and the morning.

He thought of Buffy. He wondered if she was safe; he cursed himself for his helplessness.

The sun angled across the floor, leaving him only a small patch of safety. With every passing minute, it crept closer.

Angel was sweating. His body was wracked with pain.

He closed his eyes and tried to envision the darkness.

CHAPTER 13

Giles paced restlessly in front of Buffy and Kendra, trying to make sense of the situation.

"Your watcher is Sam Zabuto, you say?" he asked this new Slayer.

Buffy watched with interest. Kendra seemed strangely subdued in Giles's presence, almost subservient. Even her voice held a touch of reverence as she answered his question.

"Yes, sir."

"We've never met," Giles went on, "but he is very well respected."

"What?" Buffy broke in. "So he's a real guy? As in, nonfictional?"

Giles ignored her. "What are you called?" he asked Kendra.

"I am the Vampire Slayer," Kendra replied.

Buffy sounded irked. "We got that part. He means your name."

"Oh." Kendra nodded. "They call me Kendra, only. I have no last name, sir."

Buffy rolled her eyes. "Can you say—stuck in the eighties?"

"Buffy, please." Giles frowned. "There has obviously been some kind of misunderstanding here."

Everyone turned as Willow came into the library. She stopped just inside the door and smiled.

"Hey—"

Before Willow could finish her sentence, Kendra advanced on her, ready to attack.

"Identify yourself!" Kendra ordered.

"Back off, Pink Ranger." Buffy's look was withering. "This is my friend."

"Friend?" Kendra demanded.

"You know. Person you hang with? *Amigo?*"

Kendra looked annoyed. "I—I don't understand."

Again Buffy rolled her eyes, turning this time to Giles. "You try. I'm tapped."

"Kendra," Giles said patiently. "There are a few people, civilians if you will, who know Buffy's identity. Willow is one of them. And they also spend time together. Socially."

Kendra was taking all of this in. She understood what was being said, but she was still very much puzzled by the concept.

"And you allow this, sir?" she finally asked.

"Well," Giles stammered, "you see—"

"But the Slayer must work in secret," Kendra broke in. "For security—"

"Of course. With Buffy, however, it's . . ." Giles looked momentarily at a loss. "Some flexibiity is required."

"Why?"

"Hi, guys," Willow said quickly, putting an end to the discussion. "What's going on?"

"There's been a big mix-up," Buffy replied.

"It seems that somehow, another Slayer has been sent to Sunnydale," Giles added.

Willow looked from one of them to the other. "Is that even possible? I mean, two Slayers at the same time?"

"Not that I know of." Giles took off his glasses, gazing down thoughtfully. "The new Slayer is only called after the previous Slayer has died—"

Giles's head came up. He shoved his glasses back onto his nose.

"Good Lord," he mumbled. "You *were* dead, Buffy."

"I was only gone for a minute," Buffy sounded defensive.

"Clearly, it doesn't matter *how* long you were gone," Giles concluded. "You were physically dead, causing the activation of the next Slayer."

"She . . . died?" Now Kendra really did look lost.

"Just a *little,*" Buffy insisted.

"Yes, she drowned," Giles explained. "But she was revived."

"So there really *are* two of them?" Willow stared at Giles, who finally managed a nod.

"It would appear so. Yes."

He sat down, stunned. He pressed one hand to his forehead.

"We have no precedent for this," he mumbled. "I'm quite flummoxed."

"What's the flum?" Buffy piped up. "It's a mistake. She isn't supposed to be here. She goes home." Turning to Kendra, she added, "No offense. But I'm not dead, and it's a teeny bit creepy having you around."

Kendra stood her ground. "I cannot simply leave. I was sent here for a reason. Mr. Zabuto said all the signs indicate that a very dark power is about to rise in Sunnydale."

"He's quite right," Giles admitted. "I'll need to contact him."

"So what was your plan for fighting this dark power?" Buffy asked Kendra. "Just sort of attack people till you found a bad one?"

Kendra sounded indignant. "Of course not."

"Why the hell did you jump me?"

Kendra hesitated. Then sheepishly she said, "I thought you were a vampire."

A silent look passed around the room.

"Ooh," Buffy quipped, "a swing and a miss for the rookie."

"I had good reason to think you were," Kendra justified herself. "Did I not see you kissing a vampire?"

Willow burst to Buffy's defense. "Buffy would never do that! Oh—" Flustered, she turned to Buffy. "Except for—that sometimes you do that." She stopped again, this time looking at Kendra. "But only with Angel," she insisted. She thought a minute. She looked at Buffy. "Right?

"*Yes, right,*" Buffy said. She tried to explain to Kendra. "You saw me with Angel. He's a vampire, but he's good."

"Angel?" Kendra echoed. "You mean Angelus? I've read of him. He is a *monster.*"

"No," Giles broke in mildly, "no, he's good now."

"Really." Willow gave an emphatic nod.

"He had a gypsy curse," Buffy added.

"Oh." Kendra stared at Buffy. "He had a what?"

"Just trust me. Angel's on the home team now. Wouldn't hurt a fly."

"I cannot believe you," Kendra argued. "He looked to me like just another animal when I—"

She stopped. Noting her strained expression, Buffy eyed her worriedly.

No. No, no, no . . .

"When you what?" Buffy asked her. "What did you do to him?"

Kendra didn't answer right away. "I . . ."

"What did you *do?*"

Angel's patch of shadow had dwindled down to a mere sliver.

As he lay there moaning softly, he tried to rearrange his jacket over his head, taking what little protection it provided. In spite of that, he was literally smouldering now, and the pain was almost more than he could bear.

The stench of scorched flesh hung in the room.

As sunlight flooded the storage area, Angel prepared to die.

He was too far gone to notice when the door slammed open . . . too weak to look up when a pair of hands grabbed his legs and began to pull.

Willy dragged Angel through the dirt of the stockroom. He pulled him away from the light and into the next room, then lifted a trap door hidden in the floor.

Leaning down, he pushed Angel's nearly lifeless body down into the sewer. Angel collapsed in the water, and as Willy lowered himself down, Spike and his minions stepped out of the shadows to meet them.

"Here you go, my friend," Willy announced proudly. "A little singed around the edges maybe, but he'll be good as new in a day or so."

Helplessly weak, Angel was almost unconscious. Spike reached for him, but Willy tugged Spike's hand away.

"Hey, now," Willy reminded him. "We had a deal."

Spike gave Willy a look. He pulled a wad of money from his pocket and started to peel off several bills, handing them over to Willy as he did so.

"What's the matter, Willy?" Spike asked him. "Don't trust me?"

Willy was quickly counting the bills. He gestured to Spike for more.

"Like a brother," Willy responded.

Spike held the last bill up. He made Willy reach for it. And then he struck him hard across the face.

"Talk," Spike warned, "and I'll have your guts for garters."

Willy got the message. "Wild horses couldn't drag it."

Spike unfolded one more bill. He crumpled it in his hand and dropped it into the filthy water.

"Oops," he grinned. "Sorry—friend."

It didn't bother Willy to fish for his money. As a matter of fact, there was very little that *ever* bothered Willy. Still, after all the trouble he'd just gone to, he couldn't help but be curious about this particular outcome.

He paused and looked up, watching Spike's minions gather up Angel.

"What're you gonna do with him, anyway?" Willy asked.

Spike looked deep in thought. "I'm thinking . . . maybe dinner and a movie. I don't want to rush into anything. I've been hurt, you know."

He thrust his hands in the pockets of his black coat. And then he strode confidently away, disappearing from view around a bend in the tunnel.

The minions followed with Angel, leaving Willy behind.

CHAPTER 14

"**D**o you have this in raisin?" Cordelia held a lipstick out to Mr. Pfister. "I know you wouldn't think so, but I'm both a winter and a summer—"

She broke off at the sight of the weird little salesman. He was standing there beside his open satchel of cosmetics and creams, and he was just looking at her. Not moving, not answering. Just unblinking and totally creepy.

Cordelia took a step back.

"Nine ninety-nine," Mr. Pfister spoke at last. "Tax included."

"You—you said that already," Cordelia reminded him. "Do you have *anything* in the berry family?"

The salesman didn't respond. He simply took the lipstick away from her and dropped it back into his bag.

"Are there more ladies in the house?" he asked politely.

"They aren't home," Cordelia said. His fixed expression was making her nervous, *everything* about him was making her nervous. "Nothing personal," she offered, "but maybe you should look into selling dictionaries."

She stopped as a single worm suddenly appeared from under his coat. It fell to his feet and squirmed across the floor, while Cordelia backed away with a gasp.

She looked back at Mr. Pfister, who was looking back impassively at her. No emotion, no expression. *Almost like he isn't human,* Cordelia thought uneasily.

At that moment Xander came back downstairs, seeing Mr. Pfister for the first time.

"Hey," Xander said amiably. "What's up?"

Cordelia grabbed Xander by the arm. "He's a . . . salesman," she babbled. "But he was just leaving." Feeling strangely freaked, she hid behind Xander, then looked hopefully at Mr. Pfister. "Right?"

The salesman just stood there.

"Okay," Cordelia ran on. "Bye-bye. Thanks."

Nothing. Xander moved to hustle him out.

"Come on, Mary Kay. Time to—"

But as Xander approached him, Mr. Pfister's face began to ripple. To slither and squirm in the most hideous way, as though there were creepy crawly things under his skin.

Xander was appalled. He couldn't quite believe what he was seeing.

"Time to . . ." He turned to Cordelia. His voice remained calm. "Run."

Mr. Pfister was standing between them and the front door. As the two of them bolted in the other direction, the little salesman suddenly began to shift, his human form falling away as he decomposed into thousands of slimy worms. The worms immediately streamed after Xander and Cordelia.

The twosome ran past the stairs for the back door, but now Mr. Pfister had reformed as a human and was blocking their path. They had no choice but to duck into the cellar, bolting the door behind them. At once worms began flowing through the crack underneath.

Cordelia screamed in panic. Xander grabbed an old broom and attempted to beat them off.

"Find something to block the crack under the door!" he shouted.

Frantically, Cordelia began to search. She could feel worms crawling over her, and she screamed again, trying to brush them off. At last she spotted a roll of duct tape on a shelf. She grabbed it and shoved it at Xander. "I—I don't—do worms," she shuddered.

Xander shoved the broom back at her. "Cover me."

Grimacing, he quickly ran some tape around the cracks in the door while Cordelia tried to kill worms. When the door was finally secure, the two of them finished off the rest of the worms that had made it through, then waited to see if the tape would hold.

To their relief, nothing came in. For the moment, at least, the worms seemed thwarted.

Descending into the basement, Xander realized

then that the door was their only way out. There were no windows down here . . . no other possible exits.

He scowled and plopped down in a chair.

"You know," he said disgustedly, "just when you think you've seen it all. Along comes a worm guy."

Breathlessly, Buffy burst into the storage room. Her frantic eyes scanned the walls, the corners, the puddles of liquor, the shards of broken glass . . .

To her dismay, Angel wasn't there.

"Angel . . ." she murmured.

Kendra came in behind her, moving slowly about the area, carefully inspecting the floor.

"No ashes," Kendra announced.

Buffy looked up at her. "What?"

"When a vampire combusts, he leaves ashes."

"Yeah, I know the drill," Buffy returned dryly.

"So I did not kill him."

Buffy got right into Kendra's face. Her voice was cold. "And I don't have to kill you."

Once again, the two of them glared at each other. They didn't notice Willy as he stepped quietly into the room.

"Whoa," Willy greeted them. "There's a lot of tension in this room."

Before he could utter another word, Kendra charged him. She slammed him to the floor and drew back her fist for a mighty blow.

Buffy caught her hand midstrike. Exasperated, she asked, "Doesn't anyone just say 'hello' where you come from?"

"This one is dirty," Kendra replied, maintaining a merciless grip. "I can feel it."

"That's nice for you, percepto girl. But we're not going to get anything out of him if he's oh, say, unconscious."

She grabbed Willy away from Kendra. She helped him up, then she slammed him into the wall. *Hard.*

"Where's Angel?" she demanded.

Willy's voice was strident. "My bud Angel? You think I'd let him fry? I saved him in the nick. He was about five minutes away from being a crispy critter."

Buffy shot Kendra a vicious look.

"Where'd he go? Home?" She tightened her hold on Willy, and he squirmed nervously

"Uh, he said he was gonna stay underground," Willy told her. "You know, recuperate."

"Are you telling me the truth?"

"I swear!" Willy could feel sweat trickling down his brow. "I swear on my mother's grave . . . should something fatal happen to her, God forbid."

"Then he is all right," Kendra assured Buffy. "We can return to your Watcher for our orders."

"Orders?" Buffy looked at Kendra as though she'd lost her mind. "I don't take orders. I do things my way."

"No wonder you died," Kendra said.

"Let's *go.*"

As they started out, Willy ran an appreciative gaze over their strong, slender figures. And then he had an idea.

"I have to ask if either of you girls has considered

modeling," he called out to them. They stopped abruptly, and he added, "I got a friend with a camera, strictly high class nude work—art photographs, but naked."

The look of disgust they gave him was the first thing they'd ever shared.

Willy backed off. "You don't have to answer right away . . ."

But the girls had gone.

CHAPTER 15

Drusilla was wasting away.

Spike could see it each time he looked at her—at her hollow eyes and gaunt face, at her pale, white skeleton hands.

He looked at her now as he sat down quietly on the edge of her bed. Very gently he stroked her brow, her ice-cold skin, coaxing her awake.

"Ah." Drusilla's voice was hazy. She tried to focus on Spike's face. "I was dreaming—"

"Of what, pet?"

"Beautiful," she murmured. "We were in Paris. You had a branding iron . . ."

Spike smiled. "I brought you something."

Drusilla nodded, but there was no comprehension in her eyes. She stared at the place where Spike had been, not realizing he'd stepped out of the room.

"And there were worms in my baguette," she whispered to herself.

She looked up, frowning, as Spike suddenly reappeared. This time he had someone with him—a tall, broad-shouldered figure who was bound and tightly gagged.

Spike smiled a slow, triumphant smile. "Your sire, my sweet."

"Angel?" Drusilla's expression brightened. She watched as Spike threw Angel roughly into a corner.

"The one and only," Spike assured her. "Now all we need is the new moon tonight. Then he will die, and you will be fully restored."

He moved eagerly back to her bed. He helped her up and held her against him.

"My black goddess," Spike murmured, reverently kissing her hand. His lips trailed slowly up her arm. "My ripe, wicked plum. It's been—"

"Forever," Drusilla whispered.

She smiled now, pressing him closer. Their lips locked in a ravenous kiss.

Angel couldn't watch. Turning his head, he felt a turmoil of emotions raging inside him—the shame and disgust of what he'd done to Drusilla, the loathing of what she, and he himself, had become. The helplessness of his present situation. The fear and terrible resignation now of what his fate would surely be.

At last Spike and Drusilla drew apart. Drusilla fixed him with a coquettish stare.

"Let me have him," Drusilla said. "Until the moon."

Spike glanced immediately at Angel, his jaw tightening in annoyance. Angel and Dru had a past. While it was distant, during its height they'd set the Old World on fire. This wasn't something he liked at all, yet he couldn't deny Drusilla anything.

"All right then," Spike finally agreed. "You can play. But don't kill him. He mustn't die until the ritual."

"Bring him to me."

Spike obligingly yanked Angel off the floor. He grabbed him by the neck and thrust him at Drusilla, who fixed Angel with a slow, cunning smile.

Gently she touched Angel's face. While Spike stood behind her, fully enjoying Angel's misery, she ran her fingertips deliberately down Angel's cheeks. Angel refused to look at her, but Drusilla grabbed his chin and snapped his head around, forcing him to make eye contact.

Drusilla frowned, purring softly. "You've been a very bad daddy."

And she gave him a vicious slap.

Buffy could think only of Angel.

Desperately worried, she wondered how badly he'd been hurt by the sunlight, how long he'd choose to hide himself underground. She wondered if he thought of her, if he needed her. And she was still angry with Kendra.

All of this is Kendra's fault, Buffy found herself thinking. *If Kendra hadn't come here, Angel would be fine, none of this would have happened.*

She struggled to bring her thoughts back to the

present moment. They were in the school colonnade, she and Willow, Kendra and Giles—and Giles was going on about something or other like he always did.

Buffy tried harder to pay attention.

"Kendra," Giles said, "I've conferred with your Watcher, Mr. Zabuto. He and I agree that until this matter with Spike and Drusilla is resolved, you two should work together."

Buffy rolled her eyes. "Oh, that'll be a treat."

"So you believe that Spike is attempting to revive this Drusilla to health?" Kendra asked solemnly.

Giles had removed his glasses. He cleaned them off with his handkerchief, then stuffed the handkerchief into his pocket.

"Yes," he answered. "That would be the dark power your Watcher referred to. Drusilla is not just evil. She's also quite mad."

He took his handkerchief out again. He wiped his glasses. He put his glasses back on.

"Restored to her full health," Giles persisted, "there is absolutely no telling what she might do."

"Then we will stop Spike," Kendra decided.

"Good plan!" Buffy cheered falsely. "Let's go! Charge!"

Giles gave a tolerant sigh. "Buffy—"

"It's a little more complicated than that, okay, John Wayne?" Buffy chided Kendra, and this time Giles agreed.

"Yes, I'm afraid it is. Spike has called out the Order of Taraka to keep Buffy out of the way."

"The assassins?" Kendra stiffened. "I read of them in the writings of Dramius."

The look Giles gave her was slightly incredulous. "Really? Which volume?"

"I believe it was six, sir."

"How do you know that stuff?" Buffy asked her impatiently.

"From my studies," Kendra replied.

Buffy nodded. "So, you have a lot of free time."

"I study because it is required. The Slayer Handbook insists on it."

"There's a Slayer Handbook?" Willow chimed in now, while Buffy looked completely puzzled.

"Handbook? What handbook? How come I didn't get a handbook?"

"Is there a T-shirt, too?" Willow asked eagerly. " 'Cause, that would be cool."

Giles was attempting to hide a smile. "After meeting you, Buffy, I was quite sure the handbook would be of no use in your case."

"What do you mean, 'it would be of no use in my case'?" Buffy argued. "What's wrong with my case?"

Giles didn't seem to hear her. He'd turned his full attention back to Kendra.

"Kendra, perhaps you could show me the bit in Dramius six abut the Order of Taraka," he said delightedly. "I must admit, I could never get through that book."

"Yes, it was difficult," Kendra agreed. "All those footnotes!"

The two of them actually laughed. Buffy looked sideways at Willow.

"Hello and welcome to planet pocket protector," she grumbled.

Kendra and Giles moved off, but Giles suddenly stopped, turning back to Buffy.

"Oh, Buffy. Principal Snyder came snooping around for you."

"Eeee," Buffy grimaced. "The Career Fair."

"You'd best make an appearance, I think."

"Right."

Kendra looked curiously at Giles. "Buffy's a student here?"

"Yes."

Kendra paused, taking this in. Then cooly she added, "Right. Of course. I'd imagine she's a cheerleader, too."

"Actually, she gave up cheerleading," Giles began to chuckle. "It's a funny story, really . . ."

Kendra fixed him with a humorless stare, obviously not interested in *or* amused at Buffy's wacky life. Giles quickly resumed his proper demeanor.

"Let's go find that book," he said. "Shall we?"

They headed off to the library.

Stunned, Buffy and Willow watched them go.

"Get a load of the She-Giles," Buffy muttered.

"Creepy," Willow agreed.

They both turned off in the other direction, moving out into the courtyard.

"I bet Giles wishes I were more of a fact geek," Buffy mused unhappily.

Willow glanced at her with a smile. "Giles is enough of a fact geek for both of you."

"But you saw how he and Kendra were vibing. 'Volume six—ha, ha-ha!'"

"Buffy," Willow said gently, "no one can replace you. You'll always be Giles's favorite."

"I wonder . . ."

"Of course you will. You're his Slayer. The *real* Slayer."

"No," Buffy said wistfully. "I mean, I wonder if it would be so bad. Being replaced."

"You mean, like letting Kendra take over?" Willow sounded shocked.

"Maybe. It would be wild if, after this thing with Spike and the assassins is over, I could say 'Kendra, you slay. I'm going to Disneyland.'"

Willow hesitated. "But not forever, right?"

"No." Buffy cast her a teasing look. "Disneyland would get boring after a few months. But I could do . . . other stuff. Any stuff. Career Day stuff. Who knows, Willow, I might even be able to have, like, a normal life."

She sounded hopeful as she said it.

Too bad she didn't feel that way.

CHAPTER 16

Cordelia couldn't stop pacing.

As Xander sat glumly in a chair, she walked back and forth across the cellar floor, arms clamped about her chest, nerves ready to explode.

"Think you could sit down or change your pattern or something?" Xander asked sarcastically. "You're making me queasy."

"Because you're just sitting there." Cordelia turned on him. "You should be thinking up a plan."

"I do have a plan. We wait. Buffy saves us."

"How will she even know where to find us?"

Xander gave a deep sigh. "Cordelia. This is Buffy's house. Odds are she'll find us."

"What if she doesn't?" Cordelia burst out. "I'm supposed to just waste away down here with *you?* No, thank you."

She moved quickly toward the stairs. Xander leapt up.

"What are you doing?" he demanded.

"Checking to see if he's gone—"

"That's brilliant. What if he isn't?"

Cordelia's eyes were blazing. "Oh, right. You think we should just slack here and hope that somebody *else* decides to be a hero. Sorry, I forgot I was stranded with a *loser*—"

"And yet," Xander broke in, "I *never* forgot that I was stuck with the numb-brain who let Mr. Mutant into the house in the *first* place!"

"He looked normal!" Cordelia shouted.

"What—he was supposed to have an arrow and the word *assassin* over his head?" Xander shouted back. "All it took was the prospect of a free makeover and you licked his hand like a big, dumb dog!"

"You know what?" Cordelia's voice lowered now, icy cold. "I'm gone. I'd rather be *worm* food than look at your pathetic face—"

"Then go. I won't stop you."

With tempers flaring, Xander and Cordelia moved closer. They were standing toe to toe now, their faces only inches apart, and both of them were seething.

"I bet you wouldn't," Cordelia threw back at him. "I bet you'd just let a girl go off to her doom all by herself—"

"Not just any girl." Xander was deliberately patronizing. "You're *special.*"

"I can't *believe* I'm stuck here spending what are probably my last moments on earth with *you!*"

"I *hope* these are my last moments! Three more seconds of you and I'm gonna—"

"You're gonna what?" Cordelia challenged him. "Coward!"

"Moron!"

"I hate you!"

"I hate *you!*"

Furiously they paused, emotions out of control.

Then they grabbed each other wildly and began to kiss.

Bodies clinging, lips burning, they kissed with reckless passion, as neither had ever kissed before. The room seemed to vibrate around them, the floor seemed to shake. They kissed without stopping, without coming up for air. They kissed desperately . . . on and on and on.

At long last they broke apart.

And then they *leapt* apart, as if they had been electrocuted.

For a long moment they stared at each other.

"We *so* need to get out of here," Xander said, heading for the stairs.

Without hesitation, Cordelia bounded up the stairs and ripped the tape from the door.

"He's gone," she announced thankfully, and they bolted.

They managed to make it through the kitchen. But as Cordelia followed Xander into the dining room, hundreds of worms suddenly rained down on them from above. Shrieking, Cordelia raced out the front door and into the yard. She was covered with worms, and Xander ran up to her, trying to brush them off.

"Help!" Cordelia screamed. "Help me!"

Xander dashed to a nearby garden hose. He turned the pressure up as far as it would go, and then he aimed it straight at Cordelia.

This time she shrieked even louder. As the water hit her full force, she flailed her arms and hopped around, her clothes and hair hopelessly soaked. But the tactic worked—as the last of the worms washed away, Xander shut off the hose and hurried Cordelia to her car.

CHAPTER 17

Buffy and Willow stood in the school lounge amid the hubbub of Career Week. The two of them were looking at a large schedule of events that had been posted on the wall.

"Okay," Buffy sighed. "My tests say I should be looking into law enforcement—*duh*—and environmental design."

"Environmental design?" Willow raised an eyebrow. "That's landscaping, right?"

Buffy shrugged. "I checked the shrub box. Landscaping was yesterday—so law it is."

They began shouldering their way through the noisy crowd. As Buffy looked around, she suddenly noticed a familiar face—the guy she'd attacked in the hallway recently. She noticed that his hair had changed color, from light to dark, and she noticed that he was watching them—and she *especially* noticed that he was staring at Willow.

"Don't look now, Will," Buffy informed her, "but that guy over there is totally checking you."

Willow followed Buffy's gaze across the room. "Oh," she said casually. "That's Oz. He's just expressing computer nerd solidarity."

"Really? Then why is he on his way over?"

Oz was indeed coming toward them now. With eyes that were only for Willow.

"Hi," he said.

Buffy smiled and kept moving. "Told you."

She headed over toward the Law Enforcement booth, leaving Willow and Oz alone.

"Hey," Oz said.

"Hey." Willow studied him for a moment, then added, "Your hair. It's brown."

"Sometimes," Oz acknowledged. "Did you decide? Are you gonna become a corporate computer suit guy?"

Willow looked amused. "Uh, I think I'm gonna finish high school first. What about you?"

"I'm not really a computer person," Oz admitted. "Or a work of any kind person."

"Then why'd they select you?"

Oz shrugged his shoulders. "I sort of test well. Which is cool, except then it leads to jobs."

"Well, don't you have some ambition?"

"Oh, yeah," he answered seriously. "E flat, diminished ninth."

"Huh?"

Oz patiently tried to explain. "The E flat's doable, but it's that diminished ninth . . . that's a *man's* chord." He tried to look serious. "You could lose a finger."

He smiled at her. Willow smiled back, not quite sure what to make of him.

At the other end of the area, Buffy had stopped at the Law Enforcement booth. The same stern policewoman was still there, and she gave Buffy a curt nod, handing her a sign-in sheet. Obligingly, Buffy added her name. The policewoman took the paper.

"Listen up," the officer ordered, "and answer when I call your name!"

Buffy and several other seminar attendees gathered around.

"Buffy Summers!" Police Lady bellowed.

"Here."

In one swift movement, the officer drew a gun and aimed it at Buffy's head.

Buffy dove for cover as shots rang out through the room

"Get down!" Buffy shouted.

Utter panic broke loose. As the policewoman fired again, people screamed and scattered. Bullets flew everywhere, ricocheting off walls, whining through the air.

"Look out!" Oz yelled.

Flinging himself over Willow, he knocked her to the floor. Almost at once he felt a hot, searing pain as a bullet grazed his arm. The two of them landed hard. Oz lay on top of Willow, bleeding.

Buffy tried to maneuver through the chaos. Keeping

close to the floor, she crawled up behind Police Lady, grabbed her legs out from under her, and knocked her down. The two of them wrestled viciously. At last Buffy managed to twist the gun from her hand and toss it away.

The policewoman drew another gun. She pointed it right at Buffy's forehead.

Before either of them could react, a foot came down on Police Lady's hand, kicking the gun out of reach. Buffy looked up to see Kendra towering over them, her face cold with determination. Taking advantage of the distraction, Buffy immediately began pounding the officer's face.

The policewoman twisted free. Throwing Buffy off, she grabbed a student before anyone could stop her. She pointed the gun at his chest and slowly began to back up.

"Don't!" Buffy cried.

With her hostage in tow, Police Lady continued on through the lounge. Reaching the door at last, she tossed the student to the floor and beat a hasty retreat.

Kendra took out after her while Buffy ran over to Willow and Oz. Willow looked pale and shaken, and Oz was sitting next to her, one hand pressed to his wound.

"He's . . . he's shot," Willow stammered. She looked over at him, her voice trembling. "Are you okay?"

"I'm shot," Oz said. Buffy could hear a tremor in his voice just beneath the calm. He paused a moment, then looked mildly incredulous. "I'm shot. Wow. It's very . . . odd. And painful."

Kendra ran back into the room. Spying Buffy, she quickly came over.

"She's gone," Kendra announced.

Slowly people began emerging from their hiding places. Everyone looked dazed. The unfortunate hostage walked over to Buffy in total bewilderment.

"Was—was that a demonstration?" he asked.

CHAPTER 18

"**S**he was definitely one of the Taraka gang, Giles. And way gun happy."

Buffy sounded solemn as she recounted this latest calamity. In fact, the four of them had gathered in the library afterward for a detailed post-siege analysis.

"And this Oz," Giles said worriedly to Willow, "he's all right?"

Willow managed a shaky smile. "The paramedic said it was only a scrape, thank goodness—"

She broke off as Xander and a very wet Cordelia trudged in. Both of them seemed agitated and upset; Cordelia was close to hysteria.

Buffy glanced at Kendra. "Down, girl," she warned before Kendra could attack.

But Kendra was totally rooted in place. And gazing at Xander like a deer caught in headlights.

"Who sponsored Career Day today?" Xander deadpanned. "The British Soccer Fan Association?"

Giles sounded weary. "We had a rather violent visit from one of the Order of Taraka."

"You want to talk Order of Taraka?" Xander shot back at him. "We met the *king freak* of the Order of—"

He stopped talking. He stared at Kendra.

"Forgive me." Giles remembered his manners. "Xander, Cordelia, this is Kendra. It's very complicated, but she is also a Slayer."

Cordelia wasn't the least bit fazed by this news. She barely even glanced at Kendra as she passed her and sat down. "Hi," Cordelia flashed a thin smile. "Nice to meet you."

"A Slayer?" Xander turned to Buffy with a knowing wink. "I knew this 'I'm the only one, I'm the only one' thing was just an attention getter."

"Just say hello, Xander," Buffy sighed.

But Xander was staring at Kendra now. Totally captivated, he moved next to her, but Kendra immediately lowered her eyes to the floor. She looked strangely ill at ease and completely mortified by his attention.

"Welcome," Xander greeted her. "So you're a Slayer, huh? I *like* that in a woman."

Kendra's eyes were fixed on her shoes. Buffy could see that she was totally flustered.

"I—I hope . . ." Kendra stammered. She took a breath and tried again. "I thank you. I mean, sir . . . I will be of service."

Xander paused. He looked questioningly at Buffy, who only shrugged.

"Good," Xander said, backing away again. "Great. It's good to be a giver."

Giles was deep in thought. He steered the conversation back to the important matter at hand.

"This assassin you encountered, Xander. What did he look like?"

Before Xander could answer, Cordelia let out a shriek. She jumped up, beating at her hair, then shrieked again as a dead worm fell out and landed on an open book.

"Like that," Xander said.

Cordelia's voice was shrill and shaky. "That's it! I'm showering." She turned abruptly and marched from the room, while Buffy eyed Xander with interest.

"You and bug people, Xander." Buffy looked almost amused. "What's up with that?"

"But this dude was different than the preying mantis lady," Xander insisted, thinking of their "substitute" science teacher from last semester. "He was a man *of* bugs. Not a man who *was* a bug." He slammed the book shut as if that explained everything.

"Okay." Willow nodded uncertainly. "Huh?"

"The important thing is," Giles went on, "everybody's okay. Still, it is quite apparent that we are under serious attack—"

"Yeah," Buffy interrupted. "These Taraka guys are *Uberbad*. If Kendra hadn't been there today I would have been toast."

Silently Kendra looked at her, the thanks duly noted.

Giles's face was troubled. "I fear the worst is yet to come. I've discovered the remaining keys to Drusilla's curse. The ritual requires her sire and must take place in a church on the night of the new moon—"

"The new moon?" Kendra repeated. "But that is tonight."

"Exactly. I'm sure the assassins are here to kill Buffy before she can put a stop to things—"

"They need Drusilla's sire?" Now it was Buffy who interrupted, jumping to her feet, her voice urgent. "You mean the vamp that made her?"

Willow saw the fear on Buffy's face. "What is it, Buffy?"

Buffy turned away from them. She took a moment to compose herself, and then she faced them once again.

"It's *Angel*," she said softly. "He's Drusilla's sire."

"Man!" Xander burst out. "That guy got some major neck in his day—"

Willow punched him. Xander shut up. Kendra looked annoyed but managed to hold her tongue.

"This thingy," Buffy peered earnestly at Giles. "This ritual. Will it kill him?"

Giles hesitated. He met her eyes reluctantly, his tone gentle. "I'm afraid so."

"We have to *do* something," Buffy choked. "We have to find the church where this ritual will take place—"

"Agreed. And we must work quickly. There are only five hours to sundown."

"Don't worry, Buffy," Willow tried to console her. "We'll save Angel."

But Kendra couldn't keep quiet any longer.

"Angel?" she exclaimed. "Our priority must be to stop Drusilla."

Angrily Xander turned on her. "Angel's our friend," he snapped. Then he paused . . . thought about this. "Except I don't like him," he added lamely.

"Look." Buffy faced Kendra now, her voice defiant. "You've got your priorities, and I've got mine. Right now, they mesh. You gonna work with me, or are you gonna get out of my way?"

Their eyes locked and held.

The tense silence stretched out.

"I am with you," Kendra said at last.

"Good," Buffy replied furiously. " 'Cause I've had it. Spike is going down. You can attack me, you can send assassins after me . . . that's just fine."

She drew herself to her full height.

Her eyes smouldered.

"But *nobody* messes with my boyfriend."

CHAPTER 19

Drusilla was actually feeling better now.

She smiled as she took a small bottle of holy water from an old, velvet-lined box.

She spoke dreamily as she moved about her room.

She was recalling another time, a long-ago time . . .

And she was savoring the memories.

"My mother ate lemons," Drusilla murmured. "Raw."

The room was soft with candlelight. Angel lay at the foot of the bed, his hands bound to the bedposts, his bare chest exposed.

He watched as Drusilla drifted over to him. As she knelt before him on the rug.

She ran her hands slowly along his chest. The heat they'd once shared was still there—scorching and intense—fanned even hotter by all those lost, lonely centuries between them.

Drusilla felt it seeping into her fingertips, into the most secret places of her heart.

And now she took her time playing with it . . .

Just to watch him squirm.

"She said she loved the way they made her mouth tingle," Drusilla went on quietly.

She lifted the bottle of holy water. She dribbled a bit on his chest. The liquid hissed as it burned into Angel's skin. His jaw clenched in pain, but he didn't cry out.

Drusilla smiled at him, her ravaged mind drifting. "Little Anne, her favorite was custard, brandied pears . . ."

Again she tilted the bottle. More holy water poured out and Angel writhed in silent torment. Part of him welcomed this misery—*knew* he deserved it—and part of him longed to beg for release. For this was a torment not only of torture, but also of remorse, for what he had done to her.

"Dru—" he moaned, but she sternly cut him off.

"Shhhhh."

He turned his head away. For one brief instant he could see her through a flowing haze of time—that innocent Drusilla of long-ago gazing up at him with wide, beautiful, trusting eyes. And he remembered the adoration he'd seen there, the fear and confusion, and then, when it was finally done, only the emptiness he'd left her.

Angel choked on the bitter taste of the past.

Drusilla waited till he'd grown still.

"And pomegranates," she whispered. "They used to make her face and fingers all red—"

And still she tilted the bottle over his chest, and still she watched the holy water trickle out.

Angel closed his eyes and ground his teeth together. This time he nearly cried out.

"Remember little fingers?" Drusilla taunted him. "Little hands? Do you?"

Her voice had grown hard and cold. She was waiting for his answer.

"If I *could,*" Angel gasped, "I—"

"Bite your tongue," Drusilla snapped at him. "They used to eat. Cake. And eggs. And honey." She paused, her voice changing to sweetness. "Until you came and ripped their throats out—"

Another dose of water. Angel's hands knotted into fists. He arched his back, trying to twist away.

But gazing down upon his face, Drusilla suddenly saw something she'd never seen there before.

The sorrow. Regret. The endless pain of remembering . . .

Her face began to soften. For a brief instant she looked completely vulnerable, genuinely lost.

"You remember?" she asked him gently.

Angel managed a nod. "Yes."

"You remember that kind of hungry?"

"Yes."

Drusilla smiled. "You used to feed me."

She wasn't talking about food now, and Angel knew it. Uncomfortably, he looked away.

"You think you don't have it in you now," Drusilla purred, leaning close to him. "But you do. I can *feel* it."

Without warning she doused him with holy water.

Angel threw back his head and screamed in unbearable agony.

"I can almost taste it," Drusilla whispered.

And she slowly licked her lips.

THE LOADS PROPERTIES

With these overtones and dipped him a bit fishy water
And she whoope his head and smashed in names
all of emoty.

"I am rather rash at it" D'out whispered
And they easted-kicked us for.

CHAPTER 20

There was still so much to be done.

Night had fallen beneath a full moon, and somewhere in Sunnydale a macabre ritual was about to take place.

"There are forty-three churches in Sunnydale?" Giles watched over Willow's shoulder as she scrolled through the computer. "That seems a bit excessive."

"It's the extra evil vibe from the Hellmouth," Willow explained. "Makes people pray harder."

"Check and see if any of them are closed or abandoned."

Willow obligingly did so. As Giles carried a large book over to where Xander and Cordelia were sitting, he couldn't help noticing how tense they both looked. Their chairs were pulled together side by side at the table, yet they seemed to be deliberately avoiding eye contact. Both sat ramrod straight. As they diligently searched through a volume of demon pictures, Giles could only wonder at their odd behavior.

"We got demons," Xander told him. "We got monsters. But no Bug Dude or Police Lady."

Giles handed over the book he was holding. "You should have better luck with this. There's a section devoted entirely to the Order of Taraka."

Xander began leafing through the pages.

In Giles's office, Kendra was gazing quizically out at the others. Then she glanced over at Buffy, who was in the process of checking and rechecking her weapons. Buffy's face was tight and drawn—she was clearly in a silent panic about Angel.

"And those two," Kendra said, indicating Xander and Cordelia. "They *also* know you are the Slayer?"

Buffy kept her attention on her battle gear. "Yup."

"Did anyone explain to you what 'secret identity' means?" Kendra challenged, lifting an eyebrow.

"Nope." Buffy stayed focused. "Must be in the Handbook. Right after the chapter on personality removal."

Kendra ignored her. She picked up a crossbow and inspected it closely.

"Careful with that thing," Buffy warned.

"Please. I am an expert in all weapons—"

Without warning the crossbow went off in Kendra's hand, firing an arrow straight into Giles's lamp, which toppled. Startled, Kendra tried to recover herself.

"Is everything all right?" Giles called.

"It's okay," Buffy called back. "Kendra killed the bad lamp."

Kendra shot her a look. "Sorry. This trigger mechanism is different." She paused, then added in a more conciliatory tone, "Perhaps when this is over, you can show me how to work it."

Buffy sighed. "When this is over, I'm thinking of pineapple pizza and teen videofest—possibly something from the Ringwald oeuvre."

"I'm not allowed to watch television," Kendra told her. "My Watcher says it promotes intellectual laziness."

Buffy stared at her. "And he says it like that's a bad thing?"

They both turned as Xander yelled to Giles. "Here we go," Xander said excitedly, pointing to his book. "I am the Bug Man, coo-coo coo-chu."

It was indeed an ancient drawing of the creature now known as Mr. Pfister. Round-faced, meek, not even very scary looking. But a magnified detail of the drawing showed every squiggle of his wormy composition.

Xander made a face. He ran a finger down the page and added, "Okay. Okay. He can only be killed when he's in his disassembled state."

Cordelia looked up at him. He leaned over, addressing her as if she were a three-year-old.

"Disassembled," he pronounced each syllable slowly. "That means when he's broken down into all his buggy parts—"

Cordelia snatched the book from him. "I know what it means, dork-head."

"Dork-head?" Xander tried to grab the book back. "You slash me with your words."

Their tension was almost palpable. Willow and

Giles stared at them, and then at each other, completely in the dark.

Kendra looked over at Buffy. "Your life is very different than mine."

"You mean the part where I ocasionally *have* one? Yeah, I guess it is."

"The things you do and have," Kendra tried to explain, "I was taught distract from my calling—friends, school, even family."

"What do you mean—even family?"

Kendra moved slowly about the room, her face grave. "My parents—they sent me to my Watcher when I was very young."

"How young?" Buffy asked.

"I don't remember them, actually. I've seen pictures, but that's how seriously the calling is taken by my people. My mother and father gave me to my Watcher because they believed that they were doing the right thing for me—and for the *world.*" Kendra paused. "You see?"

"Oh. I'm—"

At a loss, Buffy stared back at her. As Kendra read the shock and sympathy in her eyes, she shut down tight.

"Please," she said firmly. "I don't feel sorry for myself. Why should you?"

And I thought I *had it bad!* Buffy thought a moment before she spoke. "It just sounds very lonely."

"Emotions are weakness, Buffy," Kendra said, though not unkindly. "You shouldn't entertain them."

Buffy looked surprised. "What? Kendra, my emotions give me power. They're total assets."

"Maybe," Kendra replied dubiously. "For you. But I prefer to keep an even mind."

She picked up a dagger and began to polish it. For a long while Buffy watched her. And then Buffy shrugged.

"Huh. I guess that explains it."

Kendra glanced up quickly. "Explains what?"

"When we were fighting." Buffy shrugged again. "You're amazing. Your technique. It's flawless. Better than mine—"

"I know."

Buffy bristled, but managed to keep her cool. "Still," she sighed, "I would have kicked your butt in the end. And you know why? No imagination."

Kendra frowned. She was polishing the knife a little more intensely now.

"Really?" Kendra's tone was level. "You think so?"

"Yep. You're good. But power alone isn't enough. A great fighter goes with the flow. She knows how to improvise." Buffy leaned back, surveying Kendra with interest. "Don't get me wrong, I mean, you have *potential*—"

"Potential?" Furious, Kendra put the knife down. She marched over to Buffy and leaned into her face. "I could wipe the floor with you right now."

They stared at each other. And then Buffy smiled.

"That would be anger you're feeling," she said.

It caught Kendra completely off guard. "What?"

"You feel it, right? How the anger gives you fire?" Buffy nodded wisely. "A Slayer needs that."

At that moment Xander walked in and grabbed a book from Giles's desk. Kendra instantly froze, her eyes shyly aimed at the floor.

"'Scuze me, ladies," Xander said smoothly. He looked at Kendra. "Nice knife."

As Xander left, Buffy regarded the tongue-tied Kendra with sympathy. "I'm guessing dating isn't big with your Watcher either."

"I am not permitted to speak with boys," Kendra admitted.

Buffy couldn't help but smile. "Unless you're pummeling them, right?" And then her eyes widened with a sudden thought. "Wait a minute."

"What?"

"That guy," Buffy said. "The sleazoid you nearly decked in the bar."

Kendra was puzzled. "You think he might help us?"

"I think we might make him."

Chapter 21

Angel was reeling from the pain.

As Drusilla knelt before him, one knee wedged between his long legs, he could see the dreaded bottle of holy water in her hand. She dangled it over him teasingly.

"Say uncle . . ."

Weakly, he looked away from her.

"Oh, that's right." A sly smile curled the corners of her lips. "You *killed* my uncle."

She splashed him again, delighting in his cries of pain. Spike entered the room behind her, his eyes fixed at once on their compromising positions. He wasn't pleased.

"That's it then," Spike said firmly. "Off to the church."

Drusilla looked up at him, all childlike innocence. She held out her bottle of holy water.

"It makes pretty colors," she smiled.

She got up to kiss him, but Spike scarcely seemed to notice. Right now he was interested in only one thing, and more than eager to get it over with.

He moved to untie Angel. Angel had seen Spike coming into the room—he'd seen the quick flash of jealousy and betrayal on Spike's face. And now a plan began to form, a plan that would ultimately bring about his release.

I'm sorry, Buffy . . .

Angel took a shuddering breath. He'd have to wait for just the right moment.

"I'll see him die soon enough," Spike went on, untying Angel's hands. "I've never been much for the pre-show."

This was Angel's chance. Without hesitation, he took it.

"Too bad," he mumbled to Spike. "That's what Drusilla likes best, as I recall."

Spike froze. He straightened very slowly.

"What's that supposed to mean?"

Angel looked over at Drusilla, his tone leering. "Ask her," he nodded. "She knows what I mean."

Drusilla *did* know what he meant.

She couldn't help but smile at the memory.

"Well?" Spike demanded, turning to face her.

Drusilla shook her finger at Angel. She gave a playful growl. "Shhhhhhh. Bad dog."

"You should let me talk, Dru," Angel taunted, grimacing through his pain. "Sounds like your boy could use some pointers." He shifted a sidelong glance at Spike. "She likes to be teased—"

"Keep your hole shut!" Spike yelled.

He'd had enough, *more* than enough. No need to be reminded of Angel and Dru's past together. He yanked Angel up by the throat and slammed him against a bedpost.

Angel could hardly stand, and he was in no condition to fight. Yet stubbornly he kept on, gasping out the words.

"Take care of her, Spike. The way she touched me just now, I can tell when she's not satisfied—"

"I said *shut up!*" Spike shouted.

"Or maybe you two just don't have the fire that we did—"

"That's *enough!*"

Spike's hand tightened around Angel's neck. His other hand reached for a standing candelabra, smashing it into pieces, fashioning one of them as a stake.

Swiftly Spike drew back his arm. Angel could see the stake clutched there in Spike's hand, and he steeled himself bravely, a mere heartbeat away from death . . .

"Spike, *no!*" Drusilla cried.

And then Spike stopped.

For a long silent moment he glared at Angel.

And then, slowly, he smiled.

"Right," Spike mumbled. "Right, you almost got me."

He put the stake down. He tried to compose himself.

"Aren't you a 'throw himself to the lions' sort of sap these days?" he laughed. And then he roared like a beast into Angel's anguished face. "Well, the lions are on to you, baby. If I kill you now, you go quick and Dru hasn't got a chance. And if Dru dies, your little Rebecca of Sunnyhell Farm and all her mates are spared her coming-out party."

Drusilla nudged him gently, her eyes glowing with anticipation.

"Spike, the moon is rising. It's time."

She melted against him as he wrapped a protective arm about her.

"Too bad, Angelus," Spike said smugly. "Looks like you go the hard way—along with the rest of this miserable town."

CHAPTER 22

*B*uffy slammed Willy into the bar while Kendra paced restlessly nearby.

"Honest!" Willy insisted. "I don't know where Angel is!"

"How about this ritual tonight?" Buffy said sharply. "What have you heard?"

"Nothing. It's all hush hush—"

Kendra was growing more impatient. "Just *hit* him, Buffy."

"She likes to hit," Buffy reminded the bartender.

"You know," Willy held up a tentative hand, "maybe I did hear something about this ritual. Yeah, it's coming back to me. But I'd—I'd have to take you there."

Buffy let him drop to the floor. She started dragging him toward the exit. "Let's go."

But Kendra hesitated "First, we must return to the Watcher."

"Excuse me?" Buffy stopped in disbelief. "While we run to Giles, the whole thing could go down—"

"But, it is procedure—"

"It's brainless, you mean! If we don't go now, Angel could be history."

"Is that all you're worried about?" Kendra drew herself up indignantly. "Your boyfriend?"

"It's not all," Buffy threw back. "But it's enough."

Kendra looked disgusted. "It's as I feared. He clouds your judgment. We can't stop this ritual alone—"

"He'll *die*—"

"He's a *vampire*. He *should* die! Why am I the only person who sees it?"

Kendra's patience was at an end. As she squared off with Buffy, she saw the look of pure coldness on Buffy's face. The facts had hit her hard, and Kendra knew it.

He's a vampire. He should die.

Without another word, Buffy grabbed Willy by the scruff of the neck and shoved him ahead of her out the door.

Frustrated, Kendra watched them leave. "Are you that big a fool?" she called.

Buffy looked back at her one last time. With hatred and murder in her eyes.

"Good riddance, then," Kendra muttered.

Buffy didn't hear the parting remark. Her thoughts, her heart, her entire focus was on Angel.

She followed Willy through a maze of dark streets. They were in the oldest section of town now, a veritable graveyard of condemned buildings, forgotten neighborhoods, and deserted shops. Leading her several more blocks, Willy suddenly stopped in front of an old abandoned church. He looked back at Buffy, then led her inside.

Buffy found herself in a shadowy vestibule. Her footsteps echoed hollowly across the floor, and her breathing whispered harshly into the shadows.

Willy guided her forward toward a thick bank of shadows in the corner.

"Here you go," Willy said. "Don't ever say your friend Willy don't come through in a pinch."

Buffy was right on his heels. She wasn't expecting the shadows to part, wasn't expecting the four strange figures who suddenly materialized from the darkness.

Xander's Mr. Pfister, the Police Lady, two of Spike's henchmen . . .

Before Buffy could react, they surrounded her.

Willy turned to one of the vampires with an oily grin.

"Here you go," Willy said. "Don't ever say your friend Willy don't come through in a pinch."

CHAPTER 23

The ritual was nearing its peak.

Torchlight flickered through the church, reflecting eerily off grimy stained-glass windows. Shadows crouched in silent benediction across the floor. And as Spike swung the censer, breathing in its mystical smoke, he read grandly from the decoded manuscript.

"Eligor, I name thee," Spike intoned. His ghoulish vampire face was transfixed, enraptured with the evil of the spell. "Bringer of war, poisoners, pariahs, grand obscenity!"

Angel and Drusilla stood before him. In the center of the high altar they stood swaying, face to face, tied tightly together by leather straps. Drusilla was gowned in regal black. Tilting her head, she gazed up into Angel's face, her expression wild and dreamily expectant.

"Eligor, wretched master of decay, bring your black

medicine. Come restore your most impious, murder-ous child."

With black-gloved hands, Spike lifted the relic. He pulled at the base of the cross, unsheathing a hidden dagger. Stepping up to the altar, he bestowed a malevolent smile on the couple.

He grabbed Angel's hand, which was bound to Drusilla's. He lifted both hands into the air, and his voice grew louder now, trembling with unrestrained passion.

"From the blood of the sire she is risen! From the blood of the sire shall she rise again!"

With one swift movement, Spike plunged in the dagger. The blade sliced completely through both their hands, binding them with a rush of blood and a supernatural force that flowed powerfully, frighten-ingly between them.

Angel let out a tortured scream. Drusilla writhed in exquisite agony, savoring her wound.

Joyfully, Spike clapped his hands, watching the magick sparkle and lance the air around them.

"Right then!" he announced. "Now we let them come to a simmering boil, then remove to a low flame—"

He whirled around as the doors behind him crashed open. To his dismay he could see Willy coming toward him and Buffy being dragged, surrounded on all sides by his evil minions. Spike stared at them in appalled silence.

"It's payday, pal," Willy swaggered up. "I got your Slayer."

Spike snapped out of his shock. He advanced on Willy, seething.

"Are you tripping? You bring her here—*now?*"

While the two of them argued, Buffy frantically searched the shadows. At first she thought Angel wasn't here at all, but then she spotted the altar with its grisly display.

Buffy felt sick inside.

Angel . . .

Angel was so far gone, he didn't even know she was here.

"You said you wanted her—" Willy began, but Spike cut him off.

"In the *ground*, pinhead! I wanted her *dead!*"

Willy was getting nervous. "Now—now that's not what I heard. Word was, there was a bounty on her, dead or alive—"

"You heard wrong, Willy."

"Angel," Buffy whispered.

In the momentary lull, Spike heard her. He followed the direction of her gaze.

"Yeah," Spike's voice dripped with false sympathy, "it bugs me, too, seeing them like that. Another five minutes and Angel'll be dead though, so I forbear."

He paused for a moment. His face was mocking.

"But don't feel too bad for Angel. He's got something you don't have."

"What?" Buffy asked.

"Five minutes. Patrice?"

Immediately the policewoman raised her gun to

Buffy's head. Buffy steeled herself for the blast, but the explosion she heard came suddenly, unexpectedly, from another part of the room.

The church doors burst open, one flying from its hinges as Kendra did a handspring across the floor. Before anyone could react, she smashed into the policewoman and knocked her down, dislodging the gun so it skidded away.

"Who the hell is that?" Spike demanded.

As his henchmen glanced around in confusion, Buffy shook them off.

"It's your lucky day, Spike," she said.

Kendra attacked him from behind. "Two Slayers!" Her punch sent Spike spinning toward Buffy.

"No waiting." Buffy punched him harder, spinning him back again.

Kendra moved in for another blow, but this time Spike ducked, distracting her with fisticuffs as the policewoman headed for Buffy. Stilettos popped out from the sleeves of her uniform, gleaming wickedly in the torchlight.

The other vampires closed in.

As they made a grab for Buffy and Kendra, one of them pitched forward with an arrow in his back. Behind him stood Giles, crossbow in hand, flanked by Willow and Xander who were both armed. Xander let out a yell.

"Hey, larva boy!"

Mr. Pfister turned around. He fixed Xander with a bland smile.

"That's right," Xander taunted. "I'm talking to you—you big cootie."

As Mr. Pfister started toward him, Xander raced for the foyer and shut the heavy oak door. Immediately Mr. Pfister shed his human form and collapsed into a squirming mass of worms.

Xander and Cordelia were ready.

As the worms began streaming under the portal, Cordelia jumped up to admire her handiwork. She'd spread a thick layer of liquid adhesive across the floor, and the worms stuck fast.

"Welcome, my pretties," Xander gave a mad cackle. "Mwa haa haa!"

Immediately he began stomping. Cordelia hesitated, then began stomping, too—gingerly at first, but finally with unabashed enthusiasm.

"Die!" Cordelia shouted, stomping her cross-trainers into the adhesive. "Die! Die!"

Xander gazed down at the squishy floor. "I think he did, Cordy."

They could hear the fierce sounds of battle coming from the other side of the door.

They stomped harder.

Not far from the altar Kendra was holding her own against Spike. She'd always been fast, but Spike was much more powerful. After several crippling blows he had her on the defensive, while Buffy was too busy with Police Lady to help. Buffy was using all her best moves but only narrowly escaping the slash of those deadly knives. She looked over at Kendra and yelled.

"Switch!"

The two Slayers moved back to back. As though some secret signal had been given, Buffy grabbed

Kendra by the arms, and the two of them did a tandem flip. Kendra flew straight into the policewoman; Buffy landed right in front of Spike.

"Rather be fighting you anyway." Spike smiled.

"Mutual."

The remaining vampire took a swing at Giles, knocking the crossbow from his hands. As the two of them started wrestling, Willow jumped on the vampire's back.

Buffy hurled Spike into the wall. As Willy tried to escape that way, Spike reached out and grabbed him.

"Where are you going?"

Willy's mind raced. "There's a way in which this isn't my fault."

"They tricked you," Spike guessed.

"They were duplicitous!" Willy agreed, outraged.

"Well," Spike soothed him, "I'll only kill you just this once."

But then he saw Buffy.

She had climbed up onto the altar and was clasping the handle of the knife. She was trying desperately to pull it from Angel's and Drusilla's hands.

Spike tackled her from behind. The two of them crashed to the floor.

Seeing his chance, Willy bolted. He ran past Giles and Willow, who were finishing off a victim of their own.

"Hold him steady!" Willow insisted. As Giles obligingly held the struggling vampire, Willow drove a stake through its heart. The vampire promptly exploded all over Giles. Willow hastily wiped the dust off Giles's clothes.

Willy heard the vampire scream as he died, but he kept on running. He nearly collided with Xander and Cordelia as they raced in to join the others.

Beneath the organ loft, Kendra and the policewoman were still at it, full force. As Kendra once more managed to sidestep the knives, Police Lady shoved her, sending her back into a wooden beam. Kendra scrambled up again quickly. A fine sifting of dust settled down on her shoulders, and she glanced up at the loft. She could see now that the beam was supporting the entire organ loft, and that the whole thing was wobbling dangerously.

In that split second of distraction, Police Lady lunged. She sliced Kendra's arm, drawing blood.

Kendra stared down at the sleeve of her shirt.

"That's my favorite shirt," she said angrily. Then, thinking a moment, "That's my *only* shirt!"

She came at Police Lady in a hail of blows, finally knocking her under the organ loft at the back.

Up on the altar, Spike had managed to get in a good, hard punch at last. While Buffy regrouped, he looked around at what was happening. He was clearly outnumbered. Pausing only an instant, Spike grabbed the dagger and pulled it out. Then he cut the bonds and caught Drusilla as Angel fell to the floor.

"Sorry, dear, we gotta go." Spike swept Drusilla into his arms. "Hope that was enough . . ."

Seizing a torch by the altar, he hurled it at Buffy's pals. The torch missed but fell to the floor, landing on a pile of old curtains. The pile instantly burst into flames.

He had to get Dru out. Moving swiftly, Spike carried her to the rear of the church, back behind the fire and toward the organ loft.

But Buffy had recovered now. Furiously she sprang to her feet, grabbing the censer and swinging it over her head, round and round.

She threw it as hard as she could, clear across the room.

It slammed into the back of Spike's head.

Stumbling forward, he hit the beam beneath the organ loft. A long, low groan vibrated through the air. And then the loft crashed down, burying Spike and Drusilla beneath it.

Buffy stared at the spot where Spike had been standing. "I'm *good . . .*" she said proudly.

"She's *good,*" Kendra echoed, as though Buffy's friends needed convincing.

Buffy turned back to the altar. As the others watched through the thickening smoke, she knelt beside Angel, cradling him in her arms. She lay one hand gently upon his cheek. She stroked his face, his neck, his hair, trying to comfort him, even though she wasn't sure he could even hear.

"It's gonna be okay," she promised, over and over again. "It's gonna be okay . . ."

Angel's eyelids fluttered open. "Buffy?" he whispered.

Buffy's eyes filled with tears. Kendra moved in next to her.

"Let's get him out," Kendra said quietly.

Together they supported Angel and headed for the door. The fire blazed behind them, growing in intensity, creeping slowly toward the rubble of the organ loft.

CHAPTER 24

As Willow entered the school lounge the next day,
she spotted Oz at the snack machine. His arm was in a
sling, and as he saw her come in, his face instantly
brightened.

"Oh. Hey," Oz greeted her. He took a box from the
machine and held it out to her. "Animal Cracker?"

"No, thanks," Willow smiled. "How's your arm?"

"Suddenly painless."

"You can still play guitar okay?"

Oz shrugged. "Not well, but not worse."

They started walking down the hall. Oz was having
trouble getting his box of Animal Crackers open.
Willow was trying to decide how to say what she
wanted to say.

"You know," she took the plunge. "I never really
thanked you."

Oz looked mildly alarmed. "Please don't. I don't do thanks. I get all red and I have to bail. It's not pretty."

"Then forget about—that thing," Willow nodded. She took the box from him, opened it up, and handed it back again. "Especially the part where I kind of owe you my life—"

"Look," Oz interrupted, embarrassed. He pulled a cookie from the box. "Monkey. And he has a little hat. And pants."

Again Willow smiled, amused by his avoidance tactic.

"Yeah," she said. "I see."

"The monkey is the only cookie animal that gets to wear clothes, you know that?" Oz informed her, and then in the very next breath, "You have the sweetest smile I've ever seen."

Willow was pleasantly startled, but Oz kept talking.

"So I'm wondering," he gave a slight frown, "do the other cookie animals feel sort of ripped? Like, is the hippo going, man, where are my pants? I have my hippo dignity."

Laughing, the two of them continued down the hall.

Xander was heading down the hallway, too, when he spotted Cordelia. As their eyes made contact, each one turned and headed in the opposite direction. Then Xander stopped. He turned back around and ran to catch up with her.

"We need to talk," Xander said seriously.

Before Cordelia could answer, he hustled her into an empty classroom.

They stood apart from each other—a good distance apart. Both folded their arms.

"Okay," Xander began, "here's the deal. There is no reason for us to run every time we see each other in the halls."

"Right." Cordelia nodded emphatically. "Okay." She thought a moment, then added, "Why shouldn't we run?"

Xander took a deep breath. "What happened. There is a total explanation for it—"

"You're a pervert?"

"Me?" Xander looked shocked. "I seem to recall that I was the jump*ee*, my friend—"

"As if! You've probably been planning this for months—"

"Right. I hired a Latvian Bug Man to kill Buffy so I could kiss you!" Xander's tone was incredulous. "I hate to burst your bubble, but you don't inspire me to spring for dinner at Bucky's Fondue Hut."

"Fine," Cordelia fired back. "What*ever*. The point is, don't ever try it again—"

"I didn't *try* it! Forget the bugs. Just the memory of your lips on mine makes my blood run cold—"

"If you dare breathe a word of this—"

"Like I want anyone to know!"

Cordelia tossed her head. "Then it's erased?"

"Never happened," Xander said firmly.

"Good." Cordelia smirked.

"Good!"

They fell wildly into each other's arms.

Outside Sunnydale High, Buffy and Kendra were walking toward the street.

"Thank you for the shirt," Kendra said. She was wearing one of Buffy's tops, and it fit surprisingly well. "It is very generous of you."

Buffy smiled at her. "Oh, hey, it looks better on— well, *me,* but don't worry."

There was ease between them now, a comfortable sort of camaraderie. Kendra even smiled at the insult.

"Now, when you get to the airport—" Buffy started, but Kendra knew the drill.

"I get on the plane with my ticket. And sit in a seat. Not the cargo hold."

Buffy nodded proudly. "Very good."

"That is not traveling undercover," Kendra reminded her.

"Exactly," Buffy affirmed. "Relax. You earned it. You sit. You eat the peanuts. You watch the movie, unless it's about a dog or stars Chevy Chase."

"I'll remember."

They paused at the curb where a taxi was waiting. Buffy gazed long and hard into Kendra's face.

"Thank you," she said at last. "For helping me save Angel."

Kendra looked amused, "I am not telling my Watcher about that. It is too strange that a Slayer loves a vampire."

"Tell me about it."

"Still," Kendra relented, "he is pretty cute."

"Well, then, maybe they won't fire me for dating him."

Kendra seemed to be studying her. "You always do that."

"Do what?"

"You talk about slaying like it's a job," Kendra said quietly. "It's not. It's who you are."

Buffy looked down at the ground. Then she looked back at Kendra.

"You get that from the Handbook?"

Kendra shook her head. "From you."

"I guess I can't fight it," Buffy tried to joke. "I'm a freak."

"But not the only freak," Kendra reminded her.

Buffy looked into Kendra's eyes. She shook her head and smiled. "Not anymore."

There was an awkward silence. Instinctively Buffy moved to put her arms around Kendra, but the other Slayer stiffened and stepped back.

"I don't hug."

"No," Buffy echoed, embarrassed. "Good. Hate hugs."

She watched Kendra climb into the taxi.

She watched until there was nothing left to see.

EPILOGUE

The fire had finally died out.

Inside the church there was nothing left, only smoke and ashes and blackened debris.

It might as well have been a tomb.

Yet as twilight faded into pitch-black night, a whisper stirred the air. A voice moaned softly from the smouldering ruins of the organ loft. And a pale, sooty hand began to emerge from the shadows.

Drusilla reached down for that hand.

She grasped it tightly, and she began to pull.

Her body was in full vampire form—ripe and alive, glowing with strength and good health. Effortlessly she cleared away the scorched rubble, until at last she found Spike buried there.

His body was limp and motionless.

He was hideously scarred by fire.

Drusilla bent over him, tenderly wiping the ash

from his brow. She could see now that he was still breathing. He was unconscious, but alive.

"Don't worry, dear heart," she whispered. "I'll see that you get strong again."

She felt the sudden surge of her power. With one arm she lifted Spike into the air, as if he were no more than a toy.

"Strong like me," Drusilla promised him, carrying him out of the ash in her arms.

And she smiled.

THE CHRONICLES:

EPILOGUE

Ashes to ashes . . .

Dust to dust . . .

Angel knelt beside the charred remains of the organ loft. He gathered some ashes from the floor and sifted them carefully through his fingers.

It wasn't over. Not yet.

He knew Spike and Drusilla were still out there somewhere, hidden in darkness, biding their time. And that they'd be more dangerous now than ever.

My fault, Angel thought miserably. *It's all my fault.*

He could still feel the thrust of the knife blade through his hand. He could still feel the holy water burning his chest, and the dizzy confusion in his brain, and the hopelessness of watching Buffy fight for her life but not being able to help her.

My fault, he thought again, and he choked back a cry.

Because of *him,* Buffy had risked her own life. Because of *him,* Drusilla had lost hers forever. And hadn't he suffered enough pain and regret in his lifetime without dragging Buffy into it, too?

Ashes to ashes . . .

Love was a dangerous emotion, Angel reminded himself angrily. It weakened people, clouded their instincts, made them vulnerable.

Dust to dust . . .

It could only lead to tragedy and despair.

Oh, Buffy . . .

Slowly he got to his feet.

He moved silently through the shadows of the church and slipped out again into the night.

No, love was a luxury neither he nor Buffy could ever afford.

Not if they wanted to survive.

About the Author

Richie Tankersley (Cusick) is the author of over twenty books, including two adult novels, sixteen young adult thrillers, and several *Buffy the Vampire Slayer* novelizations. Among the young adult titles she has written are *Vampire, Fatal Secrets, The Locker, The Mall, Silent Stalker, Help Wanted, The Drifter, Someone at the Door, Summer of Secrets, Overdue,* and *Starstruck*. She lives outside Kansas City with her two dogs, Hannah and Meg, where she is currently at work on her next novel.

BUFFY

THE VAMPIRE

SLAYER™

THE WATCHER'S GUIDE

The official companion guide to the hit
TV series, full of cast photos, interviews,
trivia, and behind the scenes photos!

By Christopher Golden and Nancy Holder

POCKET
BOOKS

Published by Pocket Books

1492-01

"Well, we could grind our enemies into powder with a sledgehammer, but gosh, we did that last night."

— *XANDER*

BUFFY
THE VAMPIRE
SLAYER™

As long as there have been vampires, there has been the Slayer. One girl in all the world, to find them where they gather and to stop the spread of their evil ... the swell of their numbers.

#1 THE HARVEST

#2 HALLOWEEN RAIN

#3 COYOTE MOON

#4 NIGHT OF THE LIVING RERUN

THE ANGEL CHRONICLES, VOL. 1

BLOODED

THE WATCHER'S GUIDE
(The Totally Pointy Guide for the Ultimate Fan!)

THE ANGEL CHRONICLES, VOL. 2

Based on the hit TV series created by Joss Whedon

 Published by Pocket Books

ROSWELL HIGH

He's not like other guys.

Liz has seen him around. It's hard to miss Max—the tall, blond, blue-eyed senior stands out in her high-school crowd. So why is he such a loner?

Max is in love with Liz. He loves the way her eyes light up when she laughs. And the way her long, black hair moves when she turns her head. Most of all, he loves to imagine what it would be like to kiss her.

But Max knows he can't get too close. He can't let her discover the truth about who he is. Or really, what he is....Because the truth could kill her.

One astounding secret...a shared moment of danger...life will never be the same.

A new series by Melinda Metz

Available from Archway Paperbacks
Published by Pocket Books